I

*B*AF

Toby Ma...... ....

"*I HAVE GROWN* up reading and writing reviews for these humorous books about the mystery solving sleuth, Toby Martin. As Toby's character has grown over the years I too, have grown with her. Sharing in many similarities, especially the curly hair. This was such a heartfelt way to end the "Toby Martin: Pet Detective" Era. We say farewell to Toby but we will always cherish the feisty playfulness she brought to this extraordinary series, written by an even more extraordinary woman."
— Ellie Capistrant, 16, a student at Roseville Area High School, Roseville, MN.

"*WILL TOBY MARTIN* find her 'Pops?'
She finds a Bear, and that's just tops!"
— Lee Johnson author of *Poetria Nova*

Toby Martin: State Fair Security
"*I THOUGHT Toby Martin: State Fair Security* was outstanding. I loved when Toby and Freddy dressed up as a bottle of ketchup and a knockwurst! I loved the suspense of wondering what would come next. It was thrilling from beginning to end."
— Brianna Dornan, age 10, Roseville, Minnesota
Toby Martin: Park Patrol

"*IN THIS HILARIOUS* page-turner, you step into Toby's shoes and solve the mystery along with her. Ms. Grengs sneaks in some helpful writing techniques along the way like the free writing exercise. When reading this book I suggest reading from start to finish so that you can get to the 'satisfying ending'."
— Ellie Capistrant, age 12, Roseville, Minnesota

Toby Martin: School Sleuth

"YET ANOTHER TOBY TALE that delivers a great story (along with some really handy, but unobtrusive tips about English). Way to go, Ms. Grengs, you and Toby have hit it right between the eyes again!"

— Suzan St. Maur, author of *How to Write Winning Non-Fiction*

"THIS IS A HIGHLY FUNNY BOOK in an obvious way that can't be denied. Unlike some other books, the language used isn't what you would expect to hear from a book, but what you expect to hear in real life. That factor helps you to really visualize the story as you are reading it. A fantastic job by a great author!"

— Oliver Prowse, age 10, Cheshire, England

"THIS BOOK IS FANTASTIC! I could not stop reading it and was told off by my mom for still being up at two in the morning. Also I read it three times and I am still reading the book. To put it together in one sentence: it was impossible to put down."

— Alice Dobson, age 11, Düsseldorf, Germany

"A GIRL HARRY POTTER! Toby is spunky and Mrs. Trattles is snake-like. A fun read!"

— Caleb Twiggs, age 12, Roseville, Minnesota

Dearest Lee,
You're "just tops"!
Love my Bestie! "old
love is good love"
your B4K

TOBY MARTIN:
PRIVATE INVESTIGATOR

TOBY MARTIN SERIES, VOL. 6

by Barbara Grengs

Cambridge Books

an imprint of
WriteWords, Inc.
CAMBRIDGE, MD 21613

Cambridge Books is a subsidiary of:

Write Words, Inc.
2934 Old Route 50
Cambridge, MD 21613

ISBN 978-1-61386-341-1

Fax: 410-221-7510

Bowker Standard Address Number: 254-0304

Dedication

For Henry, his mom, and for all my students and colleagues who provided me with many "Toby" moments. And for Marsha, a friend and loyal Toby fan, who was reading a Toby book the night before she died.

CHAPTER 1

Embracing My Weirdness

Two Summers Later: August 2007

"Mom, I don't have anything to wear to Patty's party!" Let me explain why that was an issue.

Patty Washington and I became buds in the seventh grade when I got a group of outsiders together and formed a club called the Pearls. Patty Washington, Su Vang, Kenny Garcia, Bobby Olson, Freddy Galvin, and I were all in the club. More on that later.

Patty lived just a few blocks away from our hundred year old farmhouse in Merriam Park, a neighborhood in St. Paul, Minnesota. *Go Gophers!* Since we lived so close and went to the same school, it was convenient to hang out. Every summer she threw a party for the Pearls and this year's bash was in two weeks.

Patty and I were decidedly different people, but still managed to become friends. Having reached puberty in fifth grade with boobs and everything, Patty was a big time guy magnet. No surprise that the girls were jealous and hated her. None of that mattered to me because I was totally out of the puberty loop. I just thought Patty was smart and funny. Imagine Patty in a red, sexy cocktail dress at our winter dance and me in the green velvet, long-sleeved, high-necked dress that I wore to Mom's wedding. You get the picture.

When I was in middle school, I could have cared less about fashion. I was a tall, gangly, nerdy seventh grader with no boobs and few friends, let alone boyfriends. I wore my red, naturally curly hair short like a boy because I wanted to fool people into thinking I might actually be a boy. How nuts was that? In addition, my hair frizzed up like cotton candy in humid weather and I had no idea how to control it. So I guess short hair made sense. Not any more! I'm still tall and my hair is still frizzy, but I've put on a few pounds in all the right places, if you catch my drift. And I'm quite happy being a girl, thank you very much.

Now that I think back, having no friends was what Patty and I had in common. Just like the rest of the Pearls. We were outsiders, kids that didn't fit in with the "popular" crowd. Su and Kenny were from different cultures: Su was Hmong and Kenny was Mexican. Freddy was overweight, Patty was, well, you know, and I've already described myself. We were called derogatory terms like Gook, Wetback, Slut, Lard Ass and Faggot. We were actually targeted for physical and emotional bullying by none other than Bobby Olson, one of our club members. He was eventually expelled for bullying and making terroristic threats and finally got the help he needed.

We Pearls have talked about what happened that year a lot, and after crying and laughing ourselves silly we've decided to "embrace our weirdness." We have stayed friends, and this party is a celebration of our weirdness and our last few days of freedom since school starts in three weeks. And I had nothing to wear.

Even I had to admit I sounded pathetic and whiny. Grandma and I had just gone shopping for school clothes at several thrift and consignment shops along Hamline Avenue. I loved shopping for slightly used clothing. With fifty bucks I could buy some unique threads. Some of the stuff even had the original price tags. I had saved my baby-sitting and crime fighting reward money, so I could splurge on some really cool clothes and accessories. Yes, I am still head honcho for Toby Martin, Ace Detective Agency now named Toby Martin and Freddy

Galvin: Private Investigators. It sounds more professional and besides Freddy deserves equal billing. And yes, Freddy Galvin, is still my best friend. And no, Freddy and I are not an item. Not yet anyway.

My favorite consignment store was Retro Rush because they specialized in vintage clothes from the '60s and '70s, my favorite decades. It was all because of Grandma and her love of the Eagles and Elton John. As soon as I heard the Eagles "Get Over It" and watched Grandma boogy, I was hooked. And then there was Elton John.

Grandma's advice: "I can get the kitchen tidied listening to 'Crocodile Rock.' You should try it, Toby. A little 'I'm Still Standing' might help you clean that room of yours."

Let me explain about Grandma. In her words, "I'm a doozy of a floozy." Unlucky in love, she's had three husbands and quite a few "finances." Her word again. She swears like a character from the *Sopranos* and has a bowling average of over 180. She dyes her hair red and rats the bejesus out of it. It's funny to think Grandma dyes and backcombs her hair to get hair that I have naturally. A favorite quote from Grandma: "Men like big hair, Toby." I have big hair especially when it's humid and it hasn't worked for me. Yet. Yeah, I'm single but looking.

Then there are the V-neck sweaters and scoop necked tops that Grandma wears. Before I actually developed, I was kinda embarrassed by Grandma's showing off her ample cleavage. Now, not so much. A few years ago, she had breast cancer and reconstruction surgery, and ever since she's been living life with even more gusto. "You know, Toby, this family has a great big dose of the joy gene and a little cancer isn't going stop us from living BIG." That's my Grandma. She understands me and I think I understand her.

At Retro Rush I loaded up on long gauzy peasant skirts, blouses with big sleeves and hip hugger pants with flared legs. I also bought a purple mini dress and a pair of disco boots. Since I was so tall, I could pull off the look, at least according to Grandma, the fashion queen. I even found a fedora hat that was absolutely perfect for my retro detective look. Both Freddy and I, now sophomores, were headed for Summit High School, and I wanted to start school with some cool clothes that "embraced my weirdness."

"Toby, Grandma just helped you buy school clothes. Wear one of those outfits. Besides the party is two weeks away." Mom yelled from the kitchen.

"But those are school clothes. Not party clothes. Big difference," I said as I walked into the kitchen.

I went straight to the 'fridge to get some juice. This might just become one of those long term afternoon yell sessions that Mom and I sometimes had and I needed to have strength.

"I remember when you went to that dance in seventh grade and came home upset because Patty Washington was dressed like a hooker."

"In seventh grade I didn't even know what a hooker was. But I do remember her tight red cocktail dress. And I was hardly 'upset.' Surprised maybe, but not upset."

"Young lady, you are not getting a cocktail dress. And you will not look like you're in training for a career in prostitution. And you were upset."

"Mom, I just want to wear something that doesn't remind me remotely of school."

My clothing style had evolved—from plaid and khaki to the vintage look that I adopted last year. I was trying to recover from my Land's End past that my family seemed to think defined me.

"How about your bright blue sundress. It looks great with your hair and eyes," Mom said as she put Ruby in her high chair. Ruby, my almost two-year-old sister, took up most of our entire family's time and attention. She was like the energizer bunny in those battery ads. She just kept going and going and going. Her latest Rubyism was, "Don't wanna a nap. Sleep boring." Boy, could I use a couple of "boring" afternoons. So she'd sleep for like thirty seconds and call from her crib, "Momma, all done napping." I should have known she was going to be trouble when, at the tender age of five minutes, she threw her newborn baby hat on the floor and proceeded to scream at the top of her lungs.

At least Grandma seemed to understand the need for a little more pzazz in the party dress department. Grandma's idea of pzazz was sequins, ratted hair and false eyelashes. Not exactly my style. I was thinking more of a short skirt and cute crop top. Since I was so tall and thin, I didn't have to worry about having a muffin top. Or maybe a short sundress that would show off my long legs. Trouble was I blew all my money on school clothes, so maybe Mom had a point. I hated it when parents were right.

Speaking of parents, Bob is my stepdad; he's cool. My real dad "hit the road" when I was nine. He went out for milk and came back on the milk carton: "Have you seen this person?" No kidding, he just vanished. Poof, gone just like that. I missed him sometimes. Pops and I were buddies. And Mom and Grandma wouldn't talk about him, so I just made up stories about where he was and what he doing.

This was my favorite creation: I imagined him living on a Caribbean island running a fishing business. You know the kind that takes tourists out deep-sea fishing. I could just see him all tan and fit, holding up a sword fish or a huge marlin, something like that. He'd be living in a thatched roof hut on the beach, and then Gary and I could go visit and catch all the fish we wanted.

Just then Mom interrupted my vivid daydream. "You could borrow my lapis lazuli earrings and necklace. That would be a bit more festive. Why don't you go up to my room and check my jewelry box. You know where I keep it."

Festive? Who even uses a word like that? Screw the lapis lazuli. Screw the blue sundress. Mom has some funky-chunky, artsy-fartsy costume jewelry that I used to play dress up with when I was a kid. I could really embrace my weirdness with some of that stuff. I've got it! I could accessorize that purple mini-dress, wear my hair up, add some big earrings. That should work.

A few years ago right after Mom and Bob the Cop got married, they decided to remodel the third floor and make a master suite complete with their own bathroom. Guess they needed some privacy. It must have worked because Mom got pregnant right away. And now we have little Ruby the Ripper.

"Thanks, Mom. Mind if I go up and look right now? I'll wear my dress and see how the jewelry looks. See you in a few minutes."

"Go with, Toby?" Ruby said as she wiggled out of her high chair. She had macaroni and cheese in her dark brown curls. I was hoping she'd have red hair like me, but I must have gotten my red hair from Pops. Bob had dark brown hair. At least she got the curls. Ruby didn't say much for a year and a half 'cause she was a baby, and then all of a sudden she spoke in complete sentences. Go figure.

"Sure thing, Rugrat, but let's first get those noodles out of your hair." I reached for a noodle, but Ruby was already headed for the stairs, leaving a trail of macaroni. Both Watson, my overweight basset hound, and Lena, my labradoodle were cleaning up Ruby's mess. They were better than Mom's upright vacuum.

"My name's Wooby, not wugwat," Ruby yelled from the upstairs hallway.

Our old farmhouse had four bedrooms on the second floor, one bedroom for each of us kids and then a spare bedroom which we used for storage. And, of course, a bathroom that we girls had to share with Gary. Boy dribbles—major Eww.

Ruby's room was the smallest and next to mine. Big Sister duties seemed endless right now because we were in the midst of potty training and, as I mentioned, the kid never shut up. I was honestly looking forward to school starting. Gary, my 17-year-old brother, had the bedroom at the far end of the hall. His door was closed as usual, and we could hear the heavy bass of his music. Ruby loved "Wock and Woll." I think she got a really big dose of Grandma's joy gene because she loved to dance.

By the time I got up the stairs, Ruby was already snooping in my room. She was going through my chest of drawers, pulling out T-shirts while wearing my new hat.

I went to my closet for the purple dress and white boots. I grabbed a scrunchy and put my long curly hair in a pony tail and changed into the dress and boots. "What do you think, Ruby? Do you like my new dress?"

"Yup. Like my hat, Toby?"

"Sure do, kiddo. Let's go accessorize." I put out my hand and she put her chubby, sticky hand in mine. Maybe being a big sister wasn't so bad after all.

The Eagles: An American classic rock band started in 1971 in Los Angeles. Grandma's house would be pretty dirty without them.

Elton John: Popular British songwriter and singer

who plays the piano and wears these funky big glasses. He was famous for singing at Princess Diana's funeral. Princess Di married Prince Charles, heir to the throne, when she was only twenty. He later dumped her for another woman. And then Di was killed in a car crash. Bummer.

The Sopranos: A cable TV series about the New Jersey mob headed by Tony Soprano. Mom and Bob wouldn't let me watch it because of the sex and violence, but Freddy and I watched a few episodes when his folks were out. It was really, really gross.

Lapis Lazuli: A beautiful bright blue semi-precious stone prized for its color. Bob gave Mom the earrings for an anniversary present. Sweet.

CHAPTER 2

Milk Carton Dad

When I got to the third floor where Mom and Bob had built their romantic hideaway, Ruby was already rummaging through Mom's drawers. Our attic, aka the "smoochie/koochie" room named by Gary and me, was an unusual shape. Two large skylights and two end windows provided outside lighting for the long center room itself. Mom and Bob's kingside bed with matching bedside tables took up much of the center with an easy chair and floor lamp on the opposite end.

The builder/architect also managed to squeeze in a small three-quarter bath. The outside walls slanted and thus provided ample opportunity for built-in closet space and storage drawers and shelves, just the right height for little hands to pry. And prying was Ruby's specialty. With the fedora covering her cheesy hair, she was happily going through Mom's sweaters while I, dressed as Disco/Hippy Girl, was happily trying on artsy/fartsy jewelry.

"Ruby, what do you think of these earrings?" I shook my head and felt the large silver hoops brush my cheeks. Ruby was way too busy to answer.

"Ruby..." I tried again to get her attention. No such luck. When I looked at her, she was trying to untie a large bundle of letters, probably love letters from Bob.

"Ruby, honey, put those back. Those are your daddy and mommy's letters." When I went to retrieve the letters, she squealed which was Ruby-speak for "Chase me. Catch me if you can." Since there was little space to run, she grabbed the quilt and pulled herself onto the bed and began to jump, letters flying everywhere.

Squealing with joy, Ruby jumped and bounced, the fedora sailing to the floor. Suddenly everything slowed down and Ruby was jumping in slow motion. I saw her jump, her curls flowing, macaroni bits flying everywhere. And then I saw her bounce to the side and I knew this was going to be bad. I tried to get to her before she fell, but I was too late, and little Ruby hit her head on the corner of the bedside table. There was a moment of silence and then screams filled the air. I'm not sure who was screaming louder.

Then I saw blood gushing from the cut on her forehead. I grabbed a pillow and pulled off the case, pressing it hard onto the wound, the blood soaking through and onto the quilt. I kept thinking over and over again: Mom is going to kill me. Ruby's dress, my dress and this quilt will be ruined. And then I looked up and saw Mom's pale face with Gary right behind her.

"Oh, my god, what happened?" Mom's voice was higher than normal. It was more like a scream than a question, and then she morphed into Calm Mom, just like that. She knew she had to take control of this awful situation.

I'd witnessed Mom's transformation before when I broke my arm in third grade. While Mom was calm and competent, I was feeling sick to my stomach.

Gary interrupted. "For god's sake Toby, I can barely hear my music over the screams." And then he saw the blood and blanched.

"Mom, she was jumping on the bed and then she hit her head. I'm so sorry," I said through Ruby's screams.

"That's not important now. We need to get her to the hospital." Mom cradled Ruby in her arms, but kept the pressure on the wound. "Toby, get me a clean towel." By this time Ruby was slightly less hysterical and had stopped wiggling.

"Should I come with you to the hospital?" I asked, handing her a bath towel.

"No, Toby, you can clean up this mess. We'll call you from the hospital. Gary, are you okay to drive?" He nodded. "Good job, hon, you did exactly the right thing."

Maybe she wasn't going to kill me.

"Ruby, darling, you got yourself a little owie. Now we have to go to the doctor so he can make you better." Ruby was now whimpering like a hurt puppy.

"Maybe the nurse will give you a sucker," I added. As soon as I said the magic word, she stopped crying.

"Sucker? Want a red one," Ruby said as she started to suck her thumb. Mom carefully took the towel away so she could take a look at Ruby's owie. The bleeding had almost stopped.

"Toby, would you please get a big Band-Aid for your sister?"

Gary had already gone into the bathroom for two Band-Aids, and he was looking very pale. He handed the Band-Aids to Mom.

"It's not too bad, Toby, but I think she might need a few sutures."

She then noticed Gary who was swaying a bit. "Gary, sit on the bed and put your head between your knees." After a few minutes, his color went back to normal.

"If you're sure you're okay, Gary, get the car and meet us in front. Toby, strip the bed and wash the sheets and quilt in the washer in cold water with the usual soap, and soak your clothes in cold water until you can do another load. The stains should come out if you act quickly."

Mom picked up Ruby and went downstairs. I waved good-bye to that little girl, her sundress streaked with blood. Ruby looked up at me with sad brown eyes and gave me a little Ruby wave. I felt awful.

Maybe I could redeem myself by cleaning up. I stripped the bedding and went to the basement laundry room. I've done my own wash for the last couple of years, so doing a few bloody sheets and a quilt was no problem. As for my "party" dress, the jury was still out. I might end up with some new duds after all.

I went to the linen closet for fresh sheets, and then went back upstairs to finish the clean-up. I gathered the letters, some of them flecked with red, when I noticed the names on the envelopes. These weren't love letters from Bob to Mom; these were letters addressed to me and Gary. From Pops!

My heart started pounding and my mouth got dry. I had to sit on the bed because I was shaking so badly. I looked at all the opened letters and cards, then counted them and sorted them by the postmarked date.

They seemed to follow a pattern of sorts. Pops sent a letter around our birthdays and Christmas with a few more sprinkled throughout the year. Mom must have read them all.

The earliest was dated June 21, 2001, just a few months after Pops disappeared and the last, just a few weeks ago.

> *June 21, 2001*
>
> *Dear Kids,*
>
> *I've been struggling with how to tell you the reasons for my leaving you and your mother. My decision to leave had nothing to do with you kids or your mom. I love you more than anything, and I didn't want to hurt or embarrass you because I was in trouble. So I took the cowardly way out and left because I couldn't face a trial or the possibility of jail. I want you to know that I'm innocent. I did not steal the money, but I knew the evidence was stacked against me. So I ran. Please forgive me.*
>
> *I'll leave it up to your mom to decide whether to give you this letter or not. I trust her to know what's best for you kids.*

*Please don't try to contact me because I'll be
moving around. I'll write every few months just
so I can feel somewhat connected to you.
Remember I love you.*

Your Pops

I re-read the first letter several times, and these
phrases kept running over and over in my mind:
"in trouble," "face a trial," "possibility of jail,"
"steal the money." What was going on?

I carefully tied up the blood spattered letters
and took them to my room where I would keep
them hidden in my closet until I could show them
to Gary. We needed to discuss a plan. Together
we might be able to figure out where he was living
now. It was curious that the letters were all sent
from Minneapolis. Either he was hiding right
under our noses, or he was using someone to mail
the letters for him.

Gary and I would have to figure it out. That's
what Toby Martin: Private Eye does best. That
and cleaning up blood. I took off my blood
spattered dress and changed into shorts and a T-
shirt that said, "I'm too sexy for my hair."

As long as I could stay Toby Martin: Private
Eye, I could avoid my anger and hurt over my
Mom's betrayal. That didn't last long.

Fedora: This old fashioned felt hat a la Sam Spade and Michael Jackson.

Sutures: Doc talk for stitches.

CHAPTER 3

How Could They?

Because I was morphing into detective mode, kinda like Mom when she morphed into Calm Mom, I felt better as I finished wiping off the blood from the end table, and started on the carpet splatters. Fortunately, Mom and Bob had chosen a cranberry red plush carpet for their romantic hideaway, so the blood just looked like dark spots. Most of it went on the bedding.

How could she? How could she keep Pops's letters from us? I needed to talk to Grandma first, Gary second, and then I needed to confront Mom. It was bound to be an ugly confrontation. I felt Detective Toby fade and Pissed-off Toby emerge.

When I called Grandma, I blurted out what happened with Ruby and what I found as a result. She told me to come over immediately.

Grandma lived in a duplex in Highland Park, a posh neighborhood just a few miles away. I could get there on my bike in just minutes, especially if I was in a hurry. Grandma would know what to do and what to say.

As I was pedaling like crazy... *Grandma has to know about Pops. Why didn't she tell us about the letters? Great, now I'm pissed off at Grandma as well as Mom. And Bob, what does he know? This is developing into a conspiracy, my very own "grassy knoll."*

I was getting angrier and angrier the closer I got to Grandma's. Not even her chocolate chip or peanut butter cookies and smoothies would help soothe a PO'd redhead.

"Grandma, did you know why Pops left us?" I yelled as I barged into the house without even knocking, the screen door announcing my arrival. Sid, Grandma's cockapoo, was so surprised at my noisy arrival he didn't even bark.

"Good afternoon to you too, Toby," Grandma yelled from her kitchen, a kitchen where we had had so many laughs and good talks. I looked around at the cheerful red and white kitchen with accents of purple and hot pink. One thing that was a constant with Grandma was her love of color and colorful language.

"Do you want some cookies and milk? I hear that calms kids when they're pissed." She went to her big cabbage shaped cookie jar, withdrew two peanut butter cookies from her stash, and handed them to me on a paper napkin. She then handed me a carton of milk and a glass.

"Well, did you know about Pops? About the letters and cards Mom hid from Gary and me? I want to know, Grandma."

She wiped her hands on her hot pink apron that said, "I'd Rather Be Bowling."

"Yes, Toby, I knew about your dad and yes, I knew about the letters. I disagreed with Laura about keeping them from you kids, but I figured the letters were her problem and her business. Once you have kids, you realize they do what they do regardless of your advice."

"That's all you have to say? Kids do what they do?" I paced around the kitchen with Sid, Grandma's rusty red cockapoo, at my heels. When I accidentally stepped on his paw, he yelped and lay down in his red and black plaid doggie bed, looking at me with sad Princess Diana eyes.

"Sorry, Sid, I didn't mean to step on you." I went to him and scratched behind his ears. He wagged his tail in forgiveness. That helped and I began to calm down. I swear I like dogs better than most people. They don't deceive and have secrets.

"What do you want to know, Toby? If I can, I'll answer your questions. No BS, promise."

So I peppered her with questions:

"What happened that made him leave without saying good-bye?"

"Did he do anything wrong like steal some money?"

"Did the cops know?"

"Did Bob know?"

"Where is he now?"

"Does he know Mom remarried and had a baby?"

It felt good to let go and ask whatever I wanted.

Grandma sighed. "Toby, there was a huge scandal at the accounting firm where your dad worked. Someone had messed with the books, and over $100 thousand dollars disappeared.

When the boss discovered the theft, he went on a witch hunt, interrogating each of his employees. One of the accountants, a man named Noah Swanson, made some very incriminating comments about your dad. It turned out that they had been in conflict since Noah was hired. He felt that your dad shouldn't have been promoted, that he deserved the promotion instead. It was nasty. After Noah made his accusations, the boss called in the authorities."

"But did Pops do anything wrong?"

"I don't think so, but he felt he was being set up and decided he couldn't risk an investigation and trial. So as I like to say, he 'got the hell outta Dodge.' After that he sent Laura an occasional letter, telling her where he was, so she could send the necessary paper work. He told your mom that he wouldn't contest a divorce."

"So Mom knows where is is."

"She knew where he was then. I honestly don't know if she knows where he's living at the moment. And, before you ask, Toby, she never divulged where he was to me. I advised her to be transparent with Bob because a relationship needs honest communication and no secrets."

"But why would Pops want a divorce if he still loved us? Wouldn't he want to fight for us?"

"Relationships are complicated, Toby. You'll discover that when you fall in love and want to get married. I'm still trying to figure relationships out. My multiple marriages and engagements attest to that. Your mom and dad were struggling in their relationship. There was a restlessness about your dad that was quite disturbing to your mother."

"'Restlessness?' What does that mean? Was he having affairs? Did he want to buy a red convertible and pick up girls? Was it some kind of bogus mid-life crisis?"

"No, nothing like that, at least not that I know

of, but your mother might be better able to answer your questions. When he left, it was the 'straw that broke the camel's back.' She felt the need for closure."

"But what about Gary and me? Didn't we have anything to say about it?"

"Unfortunately, no. What happened was between Laura and Michael; it had nothing to do with you kids. Your mom was just trying to do her best."

"Well, her 'best' wasn't good enough. She deliberately kept his letters from us. How is that 'best' for us?"

"I'm sorry, Toby. You'll just have to talk with your mom. When you finish your milk and cookies, you can put your bike in the trunk and I'll drive you home. We need to find out about our little Ruby, the Rugrat. What do you say, Toby?"

I started to cry like I was a lost little kid at MOA. I couldn't even eat Grandma's cookies.

"I don't know what to say or do, Grandma. I'm all mixed up."

Grandma put her arms around me.

"Welcome to the club, Toby. I get that way myself on occasion, including crying. And this is one of those occasions," she said, wiping her eyes.

"Let's go find out about our girl."

I scratched Sid's ears and gave him a hug. You could depend on a dog's love. And a Grandma's. Other people not so much.

Grassy Knoll: The conspiracy theory surrounding John F. Kennedy's assassination. It seemed like Grandma, Mom, and Bob were conspiring against Gary and me.

MOA: The Queen of malls: The Mall of America. People come from all over the world to experience it. There is an inside amusement part and an aquarium to say nothing of a gazillion ways to spend your money.

Bogus: False, phony. Like Pops pretending to love us.

CHAPTER 4

Being Grown-Up Sucks!

The ride home was unusually quiet. Grandma and I always had stuff to say to each other, but not this time. We both were lost in our own thoughts in our own worlds.

We opened the front door which I had forgotten to lock in my pissed off state. Since I was a cop's kid and a detective, I should have been concerned, but I figured we had two vicious, aggressive watch dogs guarding the place. Instead of two growling guard dogs, we found Watson and Lena, my friendly pooches, wiggling and squeaking their delight at our return. So much for the guard dog theory. I took the two "killers" out in the backyard to go potty.

Our house seemed so empty and quiet without Ruby and Mom. I was used to their sounds: Ruby's giggles and squeals, Mom's singing to the radio and puttering in the kitchen.

Last Christmas I gave Ruby these red shiny slippers that squeaked with each step. It was my way of driving Mom and Bob crazy, sorta like when Grandma gave me a little kid's drum set for Christmas one year. I remember watching Grandma giggle as I opened the box.

As soon as Mom realized what was in the box, she gave Grandma her "I'll get you for that" scowl. I knew it well. Weirdly enough after weeks of happily pounding, I discovered my drum head had torn. Funny thing. I always suspected Gary, but now I think Mom murdered my drum. Now I'm carrying on the family tradition as Miss Passive Aggressive.

Ruby loved those slippers and wore them everywhere. One slipper was on its side next to her high chair and the other was on the kitchen table. Now my little Rugrat was in the hospital.

When we walked into the kitchen, we saw the flashing light on the answering machine. I heard Mom's voice:

Toby,

Ruby had to have eight stitches, but then she threw up so they're going to keep her overnight for observation, just to make sure she didn't get a concussion when she hit her head. You did

such a great job. You knew exactly what to do to
calm her down and stop the bleeding. Thanks,
honey, you're the best big sister. Bob just got
here. Gary will be home in a bit. I'll call you in a
few hours.

Love you!

Grandma looked worried. "I'm going to the hospital. Want to join me?"

"I don't know if I could see Mom right now; I'm too angry. But you go ahead, Grandma. Mom could use the support. Give Ruby a hug for me and give her these." I handed Grandma Ruby's red squeaky slippers. "She might as well drive the hospital staff nuts."

"I kind of like the idea of driving the hospital staff nuts. I know I did my best when I was in the hospital."

We both laughed at the memory of Grandma making these dumb boob jokes right after her breast cancer surgery.

Here are some of my personal favorites:

What kind of bees make milk? Boo Bees

Why did the blonde have square boobs? She
forgot to take the tissues out of the box.

31

*Why do men find it difficult to make eye
contact? Because boobs don't have eyes.*

"Toby, should I tell your mom that you know about the letters or do you want to?"

"Thanks for asking, but Gary and I should confront her together."

"That's very grown-up of you, Toby."

"Right now, Grandma, being grown-up sucks."

"Tell me about it. Come here, Sweetie, and give your old Grandma a hug."

Just after I said good-bye to Grandma, Gary rushed in the back door and went straight to his bedroom without even saying hello. I knew I had to get the letters from my bedroom closet and share them with Gary, but before I gave them to Gary, I wanted to read them one more time. So I sat on my bed, reading all twenty of them, crying the whole time.

Pops had disappeared over six years ago without any explanation. The letters explained his reasons, and they seemed reasonable—to my head. But my heart didn't understand them at all. How could he abandon his family? If he were innocent, why didn't he stay to fight the accusations? We would have helped him. Then we could still be a family.

Okay, girlfriend, it's time to face the music—

literally.

Gary had grunge rock playing all the time. I walked down the hall to Gary's room, the sounds of Foo Fighters blasting. I had to knock several times before he turned down the volume.

"Gary, open up. I want to talk to you."

"No problem, Sis, what's on your mind?"

"Not much, Gary." I stared at him in disbelief. How could he be so dense? "I just spent the last few hours cleaning up my sister's blood. What do you think is on my mind? I was just a little worried about Ruby, you big dope. While I was cleaning up the mess, I found these."

I waved the letters his direction and then tossed the letters on Gary's unmade bed.

"Read them, Bro. I think you'll find them very interesting." I slammed the door.

But before the music blasted again, I heard Gary get up and take the letters.

Every time I looked into Gary's inner sanctum, I was shocked. I'll admit my room gets a bit messy, but Gary's is more like a toxic waste site. It even smells funky: a combination of dirty sox, stinky tennis shoes, leftover pizza, and that boy/man smell which can't be described. I'm not surprised at all that his favorite kind of music is grunge. I don't know how Mom can stand it, his taste in music as well as his disgusting room.

I went back to my room and tried to read, but I couldn't, so I got on the computer and tried to research a bit about the "incident" that lead to Pops's disappearance. I Googled the *Pioneer Press* web site for embezzlement stories in 2001. He left in May so I started the search in April. *Nada.*

May. *Nada.*

The same for June and July. So much for researching the embezzlement scandal. Maybe the person who actually embezzled the money confessed and Pops could come home. Wouldn't that be ironic?

I just know Gary and I can read between the lines and figure out where Pops is living. Mrs. Trattles, my favorite English teacher, taught us about inferencing. The only problem with making an inference was that you could be wrong.

I was contemplating our next step when I heard Gary stomp down the hallway and barge into my room, holding the letters.

"What the **** is going on?"

Passive Aggressive: It's like when you're too chicken to say or do what you really want and cover it up with something lame. Like when girls get mad at their boyfriends and then give them the silent treatment.

Foo Fighters: A grunge band popular with loser boys with dirty bedrooms, founded in 1994 in Seattle, no doubt in some loser boy's dirty bedroom.

Grunge: Loud, fuzzy, disgusting music with lyrics you can't understand

Nada: Spanish for nothing. Thanks, Mom, for *nada*.

Irony: Kinda like the opposite of what you'd expect. Pops expected to get caught so he ran away. Maybe if he'd stayed, he would have discovered the guilty party confessed. Surprise!

Inferencing: Making an educated guess based on existing evidence, but sometimes people can make mistakes. Like Pops and Mom.

CHAPTER 5

You Be the Man

"Just breathe, Bro. Use your words," I said, mimicking Mom's advice to Ruby when she was about to throw a major fit.

Gary just stopped in his tracks and took a few deep breaths. Maybe I'd get lucky and avoid a scene.

The pause, however, was short-lived. He was water about to boil over, a lion poised for the kill, a volcano ready to blow. I'd seen him really angry before and it wasn't pretty. Usually he broke and punched stuff.

"Can you believe this sh*t? Our dad writes letters to us and she takes them and hides them like we were little kids needing protection from our own father. Has it been five or six years since Pops took off without saying anything? And all this time he's been writing. I just don't get it. I don't understand Pops and I definitely don't understand Mom."

I don't think I've heard Gary string that many sentences together. Ever. He's like the epitome of the strong silent type.

Then just when I was expecting another verbal outburst, Gary's face got all red. He clenched his fists and looked like he was about to put a hole in my wall. Instead he sat on my bed, pounded his thighs and sobbed. I couldn't believe that my six foot two, one hundred eighty pound big brother sat there and sobbed, those manly shoulders shaking. So I just did what I'd do if Ruby were sobbing and put my arms around him and let him cry. After the sobs lessened, I thought it might be safe to talk.

"Well, we were little kids, sorta. I was nine and you were eleven when he took off. And Pops left about six and half years ago."

"Why do you always have to talk and be right?" Gary looked at me with mean, squinty eyes.

If Grandma were here, she'd say, "If looks could kill...." I couldn't help wondering if that saying referred to Medusa with her snaky hair and her killer looks that turned people to stone.

I ignored him and went on. "I remember looking for Pops every place we went. I thought I saw him one time when Grandma took me bowling with her, but it wasn't him. Then I thought I saw him once at the Mall."

"And your point is, Toby?" Gary's voice indicated that he was about to get really angry again.

"The point is: we're not little kids anymore. We can figure this out and still find Pops."

"Ah, Toby, the world famous detective will figure it out just like you always do. Don't you get sick of being right all the time?"

"I don't care about being right. Not this time. I just want to find Pops. Don't you want to see him again? Aren't you curious about what happened to him? Don't you wonder if he was guilty of stealing the money? What if he has another family? Have you thought of that?"

"I haven't had any time to process this sh*t. I'd just like to go back to my room and listen to my music and think about stuff." He took a few deep breaths and that seemed to calm him a little. I offered him tissues, but he wiped his nose with his hand and then wiped his hand on his jeans.

"We're going to have to figure out what to say to Mom and Bob when they get back."

"Yeah, whatever."

"Talk to me when you're ready, Gary. I really think we need to find Pops." I went to him and gave him a hug. At first, he didn't respond; he held his arms stiffly to his side. Then he relaxed and hugged me back.

"Thanks, Sis," Gary said as he left my room with his head down and his shoulders sagging. I had the feeling that I was looking at a much older man, not my 17-year-old brother.

Gary thanking me was a first. Gary wasn't known for his manners. Mom had to force him to write thank-you notes for Christmas and birthday presents, and she was always reminding him to be polite.

Here I was comforting my big brother, and I had no idea who he really was. All my life he teased and tormented me about my hair, my body, my detective work, my school work—everything. He was simply my annoying big brother and a Boy to boot. Not once did I ever think of him as a person with feelings.

I understood more about my brother in these past few hours than I ever had before. He couldn't bear the sight of blood and nearly fainted when he saw little Ruby's cut and then he cried about Pops. No, he sobbed about Pops. He really cared about Ruby and Pops. In fact, I think he cared about our whole family. All this time he was missing Pops just like I was, and we never talked about it. Weird. This was a whole new Gary.

Funny that I never thought of Freddy as a Boy with no feelings. He was just my loyal friend and foil. I'd seen him afraid, protective, sweet, helpful, and even loving. We had been through a lot together and I treasured his friendship. Maybe he could help figure out where Pops was hiding. So I did what I always do and called my BFF.

"You're not going to believe the day I've had, Freddy. Any chance you could come over for a snack and some debriefing? We have a mystery to solve."

"Sounds like a plan, Boss. I've been hankerin' for a good whodunnit and a meat lover's pizza. Any chance of that?"

"You must have been reading my mind, Freddy. I just happen to have a double cheese, sausage and pepperoni frozen pizza. Maybe some ice cream for dessert. Think that might interest you?"

"Are you kidding me? Throw some fruit on that ice cream and it's a deal."

"You are such a gourmand, Freddy."

"Yup, I be the man. I'll be over in ten. Over and out, Boss."

That boy definitely needs his hearing checked.

Medusa: One of the three snaky headed ladies from Greek mythology. When Medusa gave you The Look, you turned to stone.

Epitome: The best, the highest, the mostest. I

thought Gary was the epitome of the strong, silent type, but surprise, the boy was human after all. Go figure.

Gourmand: An expert in good food. When I called Freddy a "gourmand," I was being ironic.

CHAPTER 6

This is Intense, Man, Very Intense.

I just had time to number the letters according to the dates they were written when Freddy rushed into the kitchen.

"Smelling good in here, Toby." Boys, especially Freddy, loved their food. I swear that I could have been very popular had someone invented a body wash, shampoo or cologne with the scent of pepperoni and cheese pizza: Eau de Sausage. While Freddy and I were chowing down, I filled him in on what was happening with our weird family: Ruby's accident, her finding a stack of letters from Disappearing Dad, and finally Gary's meltdown.

"What does my mighty foil make of this mess?" I asked between bites of pizza. I was already feeling better about the letters and Mom. It's amazing what eating greasy junk food with a best friend can do to ease a bad mood.

Freddy was just about to answer with his mouth full, as always, when Grandma barged in the front door. The dogs barely acknowledged her arrival because they were so focused on the possibility of a dropped bit of pizza crust. "Any pizza left for an old lady?" Grandma asked.

"I'm always willing to share my food with an attractive older woman," Freddy said, grinning, a long string of mozzarella hanging from his chin. That Freddy can be a real charmer. "Mrs. Tobias, how's everything at the hospital?" He handed Grandma a big slice of pizza.

Just before Grandma gave us a Ruby update, Gary came into the kitchen, demanding a slice of Meat Lovers' Special. No surprise there. Flies to honey and all that.

"Gary, the Great, has decided to grace us with his presence. And to what do we deserve this honor?" Freddy said.

"Hey, Sis, is there another one of these in the freezer?" Gary asked as he reached for a soda, totally ignoring Freddy's question.

"I'll check, but I think we only have one pepperoni sausage combo left, and Mom wanted to save that for Bob."

"And Bob is still at the hospital so what's the big deal, Sis?" Now that was the self-absorbed Gary I knew. Gary, the Sensitive, the boy I had comforted, the boy who had cried over his father, had disappeared.

"If I may interrupt this fascinating display of sibling affection," Grandma said with a grin, "Bob will be at the hospital for a few more hours at least. Then he needs to check in at work. He'll be back for a bite of supper with you kids. Your mom will be staying all night with Ruby, so you might want to save the last pizza for Bob, unless either of you kids wants to make supper."

"Whatever," Gary said as he reached for the last piece.

"Anyone for ice cream? We have lots of that."

As I dished up big scoops of vanilla for everyone, Grandma continued telling us about Ruby. The Rugrat was feeling much better, especially after Grandma gave her the red squeaky slippers. The doctor wanted to keep her overnight as a precaution, but everyone seemed to think she'd be just fine. I grinned at the thought of the Rugrat squeaking her way through hospital corridors.

"Does Mom want any of Ruby's stuff, like jammies, books or toys? I could put some of her favorite things together for Bob to take up after supper."

"Nice of you to offer, but I don't think so, Toby. The children's ward has lots of fun stuff for the kids to play with and movies to watch. Plus the pjs are adorable. She's having the time of her life, especially because she gets red Jell-O and ice cream whenever she wants. The nurses and aides are quite taken with her."

Grandma looked at Gary and me and asked, "How are you two doing with ...you know?" I knew Grandma was hesitant to say anything because Freddy was there.

"Freddy knows everything," I said. Freddy, now in a really awkward position, stayed completely focused on his ice cream, reminding me of the dogs' pizza crust fixation.

"So much for the 'private' in Toby Martin, Private Eye," Gary said sarcastically. "Way to go, Sis. Did you tell anyone else about our screwed up family? This is family business, Toby. What don't you understand about the word family or private, for that matter."

"Freddy is family, you selfish jerk. More than you most days."

"I think I will go now," Freddy said, getting up from his chair. "Awkward," he whispered to me. I got up to go with him.

"Wait a minute, kids, let's think this through,"

Grandma said, giving Gary her "Don't mess with me stare."

"Freddy and Toby are detectives, and if you are determined to find your dad, it seems that they should be on the case. They do have lots of experience and are good at finding clues."

"Whatever," Gary said as he shoveled in the ice cream. After a few slurpy silences, Gary said, "So, Toby, do you and your trusty sidekick have a plan?"

"Actually we do."

Freddy looked at me with a confused look on his face. He mouthed, "We do?"

"Grandma, why don't you tell Gary and Freddy what you know about Pops's disappearance?"

"You mean you knew about this too? I can't believe you had information and kept it from us." Gary was ready to blow again. Grandma just looked tired and sad.

"I felt like that too, Gary, but Grandma was in a bad spot. She promised Mom to keep the secret, and she tried to convince her to talk to us and share the letters. So if we're going to be mad at someone, it should be Mom not Grandma. Just let her talk, okay?" Gary stopped pacing and looked at me.

"When did you two have time to ... you know."

"I found the letters after Ruby had her accident, and you were at the hospital with Mom and Ruby.

I was really, really pissed off and didn't know what to do, so I called Grandma and rode my bike over there. I had tons of questions and she answered them. So just let her talk, Gary." He sat down at the table and seemed to be ready to listen.

"Whatever." When Gary said that, I knew he was calming down a bit. Grandma patted his hand.

"Here's what I know: There was a huge scandal where your dad worked and $100 thousand dollars went missing. A man named Noah Swanson went to the boss and said that your dad might be the one responsible. Apparently he was angry that your dad had gotten the promotion he wanted. Anyway your dad thought he was getting set up to take the fall and decided to leave town to save you the embarrassment and shame of an investigation and trial. He and your mom were having problems, and this was the last straw for Laura. Apparently it was the last straw for him as well. She filed for divorce and he agreed to it."

"Then Mom knew where to send the divorce papers, right?"

"Yes, she did, but I don't know where that was. You'll have to ask her."

"Oh, that reminds me. I did try to research embezzlement cases around that time, but couldn't find anything. Maybe someone confessed and the crime was solved without an investigation or trial. Wouldn't it be something if Pops was innocent? He could come home."

"It could also have been a huge bookkeeping mistake. I don't know, honey, what actually happened. The scandal seemed to vaporize after your dad left."

"Maybe Bob could help us out there. We can ask him when he gets home."

"I wouldn't want to be Bob tonight or your mom tomorrow morning. This is intense, man, very intense," Freddy added. "Any one want another soda?"

"Actually, I'd like a glass of wine," Grandma said as she went foraging in the fridge.

"Me too," I said, though I didn't drink.

"Me three," Gary said, though he didn't drink.

"Me four," Freddy joined in, though Freddy didn't drink either.

"In your dreams, kids," Grandma said as she poured her Chardonnay.

"I've read through the letters twice and I'd guess Gary has too." I looked at Gary and he nodded in agreement.

"I've wondered about a few things." Gary nodded again.

"Grandma, why don't you start reading them aloud. I've numbered them according to date written. If there's a word or a phrase that stands out or if we have questions, we can write them down along with the letter's number. Mrs. Trattles told us that we need to look at nouns and verbs for clues when we make inferences. We can then compare notes at the end. When Mom gets home tomorrow morning, we can ask for her help."

I looked at Gary when I mentioned Mom, and he kinda curled his lip like Watson did when he was feeling aggressive. There were lots of unresolved issues with Mom that we needed to talk through. And then there was Pops.

"Get some paper and pencils, Toby, and let's figure out where Michael is hiding. Just one thing, kids: Are you prepared to find out the truth? It might get ugly and you might end up getting hurt again."

"Now that we've read the letters, we can't go back now can we, Gary?"

"Nope; you're right about that, Sis. Let's find him. I've got a few things I want to say to the jerk. And to Mom as well."

"Me, too."

"Me, three," said Grandma. Freddy was silent.

Eau de (toilette): The French translation is toilette water (*eau*), but toilette refers to personal bathing or washing. It's aromatic water, not quite as strong as cologne or perfume. Now the dogs love a drink of *eau de* toilet.

CHAPTER 7

Gobsmacked and Hoodwinked

After about an hour of listening to the letters one more time, we came up with the following list of words that might give us clues as to Pops's location: *granite, hospital, quarries, camping, Jim, Marie, Madeline, apples, Mission Hill, Boundary Waters, wood working, mulligan, lake effect snow, custard, dog sledding, library, wolves.*

"I think we can conclude he's somewhere 'up north,'" Grandma said after reading the letters out loud. "Somewhere near the Boundary Waters. Get your laptop, Gary, and let's do some research." Gary bounded upstairs and quickly returned with his laptop. I think we all felt better once we started doing something.

"Look up Boundary Waters, Gary," I suggested, realizing too late that I was stating the obvious. I've got to learn not to blurt out whatever crosses my pathetic brain.

"Duh, Sis, I'm not a complete idiot," Gary glared at me.

"Sorry, Bro, just excited."

Then he started reading: "Superior National Forest, between Canada and the U.S., glaciers, cliffs, canyons, blah, blah, blah."

"Try towns close to the Boundary Waters next, honey," Grandma suggested.

"Aha...Ely and Grand Marais," Gary said. "Now I'll Google each of them. Hmm..."

We all jumped up and surrounded him, reading over his shoulders.

"Guess we can cross off a few of those words like camping, dog sledding, wolves and lake effect snow, because they all connect to Lake Superior," Gary said.

"Although dog sledding and camping could connect to just about anywhere in Northern Minnesota," Grandma added. "But let's focus on the Boundary Waters for the moment. We've got to start somewhere."

"Oh, don't forget to cross off Boundary Waters," I said. Rats! I did it again. This time Gary just looked at me like I was one of Watson's poop piles.

"Granite sounds like it might mean something. Hey, wait a minute, isn't St. Cloud the Granite City? I remember my cousin went to St. Cloud State and my dad teased him about going to the granite quarries to 'make out' with his girlfriend," Freddy said after being quiet for the last half hour.

"Hmm...I'll have to remember that if I decide to go to St. Cloud State. Any ideas about the people mentioned?" Gary asked.

"Could be friends. Maybe Pops has a girlfriend?" I asked, not wanting that to be the case at all.

"Or two," Freddy piped up. I glared at him. I liked him better when he was quiet.

"Let's leave the proper nouns for now and focus on the others," Grandma said. "I think the food references are too general to give us much information, same with hospital and library. I'm sure St. Cloud, Ely, and Grand Marais have libraries and I know St. Cloud has a hospital. Maybe there's a mention of medical facilities on the Ely and Grand Marais web sites." We were all quiet while Gary typed away.

"Yup, both towns have hospitals: Ely-Bloomensen Community Hospital..."

"Bet that's in Ely," I interrupted. This time Gary laughed. "Good one, Sis."

"And there's the Cook County North Shore Hospital in Grand Marias."

"That leaves mulligan," Grandma said. "I never knew your dad was into golfing."

"What's a mulligan anyhow? Never heard of it," I said.

"It means you can do a shot over. It's mostly used on the first hole on the first drive, when people are generally nervous about making a fool of themselves."

"I love the idea of do-overs in sports," I said, thinking of all the times I screwed up free throws when I went out for basketball in eighth grade. My basketball career lasted for one season. I would have quit after the first game, but Bob and Mom wouldn't let me. Coach Bruno thought that because I was so tall I'd be good. Guess I showed her! You'd think with a name like Bruno she would have been mad, but she wasn't. She told me I was good for team morale because I could get everyone laughing. Maybe I should have tried out for team mascot.

"What do you think he meant when he said he needed a mulligan?"

"I think your dad was wishing he could have a do-over with you kids. Maybe even with his job."

On that note Bob walked in the door. We swarmed him with questions about Ruby. When he explained that she was just fine and having fun with the other kids and the nurses, we decided it was time to ask questions about Pops.

"This looks like quite the party, kids. What's goin' on?" Bob went to the 'fridge to get himself a beer. "Another Chardonnay, Eloise?"

"No, I'm good. The kids have some questions about Michael that maybe you could help answer."

"Where did that come from?" Bob looked a bit confused, so I explained about finding the letters and having the conversation with Grandma.

"Oh, I see," he said, taking a slug from his beer. Usually he just sipped his beer, but this time he took a gulp. I could tell he was "gobsmacked" as the Brits say on TV. "What do you already know?"

"Guys, I think you need some privacy. I'll talk to you later, Toby. Thanks for the pizza," Freddy said as he left by the back door.

"Call ya," I said.

Gary and I explained what we learned from the letters and Grandma.

"Why couldn't I find any info on the embezzlement?" I asked.

"That's because it was settled out of court. Your father was exonerated, by the way, but by the time the guilty party confessed, Michael had pretty much disappeared. Apparently this Noah Swanson had second thoughts about his accusations. When he found out Michael left his family because of him, he felt guilty and re-examined the evidence. He found his mistake and found the real embezzler. He was man enough to tell his boss and the rest is history."

"You mean Pops didn't do it?"

"Yup, that's what 'exonerated' means, Sis."

"He didn't do it." I kept saying that over and over again. What a relief—like finding out a major project due date was extended or that school was canceled on the day you were scheduled to give a big speech. I must have deep down believed he might be guilty. That really, really made me feel rotten—that I'd doubted Pops.

"Don't deny it, Gary. You had your doubts as well," I said. Gary just looked at his pizza crust. He probably felt ashamed like I did.

"We all had out doubts, Toby. I wonder why Laura didn't share that he was exonerated with me?" Grandma asked.

"Not a clue," Bob said.

"Poor Pops, he ran away for nothing. We have to find him and tell him. Why didn't Mom tell him he'd been cleared?"

"Here's what I know. Laura knew where Michael was when she filed for divorce. He was living in St. Cloud somewhere on the north side of town. You'll have to ask your mother for the address. When she found out he'd been cleared of all charges, she wrote to him, but the letter came back stamped 'Address unknown.' He'd already left town."

Freddy was right about St. Cloud and the quarries.

"Then the letters and cards started coming postmarked from Minneapolis. She concluded that someone he knew was taking his letters to Minneapolis, an effort to keep his whereabouts hidden. You have no idea how Laura waited for the mail to arrive every day. When you kids were in school, no problem, but the summers were hell if you were home. She was constantly worried you'd get the mail and find the letters. After a few years, the letters came at more scheduled times like birthdays and Christmas, so that eased her stress a bit."

"If she didn't want us to see the letters, why did she keep them?"

"Good question, Gary," I said. We were both hoodwinked by Mom, Pops, and to some extent Grandma and Bob. It felt like Gary and I were all alone in this. No one else cared. We had to find Pops.

"Laura and I disagreed about the letters, but it was ultimately her choice. She was planning to give you the letters when you were old enough to understand."

"Understand what? The fact that she didn't want us to have a relationship with our father?" I was getting royally pissed off again.

"It was complicated because the divorce wasn't just about the accusations of embezzlement; it was also because of the relationship and I think that's what she was hoping you'd come to understand."

"Whatever," Gary said. "I'm done with this conversation." He left to go to his inner sanctum.

"Me too," I said, taking the dogs' leashes. "I'm so outta here." As I exited the front door with two very excited dogs, I could hear Gary's grunge rock blasting angrily through the house.

Gobsmacked: British for flabbergasted. Gob refers to mouth and when something like finding Pops's letters causes you to gasp and put your hand over your mouth, you've been properly gobsmacked.

Hoodwinked: Scammed, deceived, tricked. All three apply to Mom's hiding the letters from us kids.

CHAPTER 8

"Da Plan, Boss, Da Plan."

When I got back from my three mile walk, Grandma was gone, and Bob was talking to Mom on the phone, the Twins game providing the background noise. I unleashed the dogs and gave them their customary post walk treat. Lena settled down in her bed and Watson waddled off.

I stopped for a dish of ice cream, my post walk treat, and then went up to Gary's room. He was sprawled across his bed, reading a magazine. I took a deep breath, the last good air I would breathe for awhile, and entered Gary's stinky man cave.

"We need to agree on a plan," I said, looking around for a place to sit, but Gary was sprawled on his bed and his desk chair was covered with dirty clothes. I kicked away clothes and some garbage and sat down on the grungy carpet. Eww. Good thing I was up to date on my shots.

"Da plan, Boss, da plan," Gary said, laughing. Laughing, definitely a good sign that he was feeling better. We used to watch this dumb show called *Fantasy Island* and this midget named Tattoo would point to the sky and say, "Da plane, Boss, da plane."

"Pretty funny, Bro. I remember watching those reruns." I put my hand down on the carpet and it felt sticky. "This carpet is super gross and it stinks. Any place else I could sit?"

Gary pointed to a mound of clothes in the corner. "Use the bean bag." I had no idea that Gary even had a bean bag. "Just throw the clothes on the floor."

Out of the corner of my eye I saw the clothes move. Ohmigod!

"Gary, the chair is moving! I think it's a rat!"

"I bet it's the snake I brought home from the biology room. I lost it a couple of days ago!"

"You're the rat! You don't even take biology. You used that snake line last year and I fell for it! I'm not falling for that again."

Gary just snorted in delight. Then I saw something black, wet and shiny wiggle. It had to be the snake. I screamed. Gary laughed and then Watson slowly emerged nose first from the pile, shaking off the clothes, and wiggling all over when he saw me.

"Watson, you scared me half to death. I almost peed my pants." I took several deep breaths, trying to regain what little dignity I had left. I glared at Gary. To think I was planning two weeks with him on a road trip. I must be nuts.

"It wouldn't be the first pee on this floor. When Lena was a pup, she let 'er rip a couple of times right where you were sitting."

"Great. Now could we get back to the plan?"

"Spill it, Sis."

"You agree we need to find Pops, right? We've got to tell him it's safe to come home and visit once in a while. Right?" Gary nodded in agreement.

"Well, when Mom and Bob get back from the hospital tomorrow morning, we should be packed and ready to go on our little road trip. We just have to figure out a way to convince Mom that we need to find Pops. Bob is on the phone as we speak, talking to Mom, spilling the beans. So she shouldn't be completely gobsmacked when we ask to go on our trip."

Gary rolled his eyes. "Too much PBS, Sis?"

"Right. We give her our thoughtful reasons for the trip, making sure she knows we'll be safe because that's always Mom's big concern. We'll check in with our phones once or twice a day. And we'll take Lena along as our special protector. We'll remind her that you're a good driver and that we'll be very careful with the car. We'll promise we won't pick up hitch hikers."

"What about money for gas, food, and motels?"

"Ouch, forgot about that." I slapped my forehead like they do in the V-8 TV commercial.

" How much do you have?"

"I'll check." Gary walked over to his dresser, opened his top drawer and pulled out a rubber snake that he threw at me. I screamed again. He laughed again. "Works every time."

"How many times have you thrown that stupid fake reptile at me? Grow up!" I was tempted to stomp out and slam the door, but someone had to be the adult here. We had to find Pops.

"Are you finished being a jerk? We have to plan our strategy."

"Right you are, Sis. I need to count my cash." Then he pulled out a sock that was filled with cash.

"Seriously, Gary, a sock?" Guess that's where the phrase "sock it away" comes from.

"I have about $60 bucks. And you?"

I knew exactly how much money I had because I kept close track of my finances. I must have the accountant gene just like Pops. "About $50 dollars. I would have had more, but I went school clothes shopping with Grandma."

"Look, $110 dollars won't be enough for two weeks on the road. Gas alone is almost three bucks a gallon and we'll be driving a lot of miles."

"Two weeks! That's a long time to be gone. How do you figure?"

"Well, we've got St. Cloud to investigate which shouldn't take too long once we find the address. We'll just show them the picture and ask if they have any idea where he's gone. Since we're in St. Cloud, I'd like to cruise the campus. In case I decide to go there. If we don't get any leads, we'll head up to Ely. If that's a dead end, we'll hit Grand Marais. After that who knows? We can't be gone much longer because of school and then there's my part-time job at the State Fair."

"And I've got Patty's party in two weeks. We need to convince Mom that two weeks will be enough time to find Pops. And if we don't find him, we'll come home, no arguments."

"We still need more money, Sis. I don't feel right about asking Bob or Mom for money."

"Me either. I'll ask Freddy for a loan. He owes me anyway for the last couple of movie dates. Two weeks is a long time, and we'll have to be very careful not to overspend. We can sleep in the car if we need to and load up a cooler with sandwiches and drinks. We'll take dog food with us. We'll need a good picture of Pops and the St. Cloud address, a good map of Minnesota..."

"Take a breath, Sis. We'll figure it out."

"Gary, we are doing the right thing, aren't we? I'm kinda scared. What if Pops has another family? What if he doesn't really want us in his life anymore?"

"Guess that's what this little road trip is all about. Both Bob and Grandma are on our side; they didn't agree with Mom. It's Mom we have to convince. You have a good plan, Sis. Sure hope it works out."

"What if she says we can't go?"

"We'll find out tomorrow. Bob will bring them home sometime late tomorrow morning after the doctor releases Ruby. We should make sure Grandma is here; she can always talk sense to Mom even if we can't. Until then, you'll just have to chill."

"You too, Bro. I'm going to call Freddy and then Grandma. Then I'm going online to find out where Ely is and how to get there. Maybe I can map out our route, so we don't spend time getting lost. We can talk strategies while you drive. And, Gary, please leave your Foo Fighters CDs home. We can listen to the radio."

"Like I said, Sis, you'll just have to chill."

"Don't you dare pack that stupid rubber reptile either! I mean it, Gary."

He just laughed, pushed me out the door and turned up the grunge.

Fantasy Island: On a remote, but beautiful, island, resort owner Mr. Roarke with his trusty sidekick, Tattoo, made his guests' dreams come true...or not.

PBS: Public Broadcasting Service. I used to think it was nerdy to watch Channel Two, but I discovered *Masterpiece Theatre* and *Mystery,* both totally awesome programs

CHAPTER 9

Patty Cakes, Brekkie and Basilisks

I was in bed, breathing hard. I couldn't move. I felt powerless, trapped. My heart was pounding like I had just finished running a race, but I couldn't move. Then I heard a rustling sound, like a snake slithering through dry leaves. I opened one eye and then the other. Across the room, I saw a moving pattern of browns, greens and grays pulsate toward my bed. The rustling and hissing got louder and the form continued to come closer. Then it slithered up the side of my bed and crawled up my leg, its heavy form pinning me to the mattress. It opened its mouth. . .

"Toby, I want some brekkie."

I awoke with a start, my scream morphing into a croak, and I saw the cutest kid ever, her dark curly hair matted on one side. Ruby is so not the Basilisk.

I must have overslept. Sure enough I looked at my alarm clock and it was almost ten.

"Toby, wanna see my owie?" She pushed her curls aside and showed me a neatly sutured cut and a bump. "They used a 'rrrr' and my curls went 'all gone.' Mama holded me so I wouldn't be afeared."

"I'm so proud of you, my brave little rugrat." Ruby grinned. "Now I need a hug." It felt wonderful to feel her sticky fingers on my arm. Finally, my heartbeat slowed, and I relaxed after my Harry Potter nightmare. That darn Gary and his stupid rubber snake.

"Come on, Toby. Gamma's here and Mama making patty cakes." She clapped her hands.

When Ruby was about nine months old, she loved to play patty cakes. I would put her on the bed and I'd sing: "Patty cakes, Patty cakes, Baker's man/ Put 'em in the oven as fast as you can/ Roll 'em and roll 'em and mark 'em with a T/ and put 'em in the oven for Ruby and me."

She'd clap her hands and giggle. When I'd sing the "Roll 'em" line, I'd push her on her back and gently roll her tummy like I was kneading bread and she would squeal. Somehow she connected pancakes with patty cakes. From then on, our entire family called pancakes patty cakes.

After that trip down memory lane, I suddenly remembered all that happened yesterday. The letters, the road trip, the conversations, all crashed into me, like the time this huge girl slammed into me on the way to the basket. After I got off my duff, I got to throw a couple of free throws. Maybe patty cakes were my free throws. Just as long as Mom and I didn't get into it.

"Well, Ruby-cakes, let's go get Gary and have ourselves some brekkie." Ruby and I walked hand in hand to Gary's room. His door was open, his bed made, his room sorta clean, and his suitcase packed. What was going on?

As we walked down the stairs, I heard laughter from the kitchen. Laughter, usually a good sign.

"So the princess is finally awake!" Grandma looked surprisingly perky and well-rested, sitting at the kitchen table with Gary, drinking coffee. Alongside her chair were bags of groceries. Curious. Mom was cooking, at least her version of cooking. The sausage was heating in the microwave and the frozen patty cakes were on the counter ready to pop into the toaster. Bob had evidently gone to work.

"Kinda hard to sleep with all this noise going on." I didn't mention that I was nearly eaten by a Basilisk.

"Before we start eating breakfast, I need to clear the air. Toby, I'm so sorry about the letters and not sharing them. I was wrong. I should have listened to Grandma and Bob. You and Gary are mature enough to handle what happened to me and your dad. You impress me every day with your common sense like how you handled yesterday's accident. I am so grateful for both of you. Can you forgive me?"

I ran to Mom and gave her a big hug. I looked over my shoulder at Grandma who winked. By this time, Ruby, wide-eyed from the family drama, had crawled into Grandma's lap.

"Why Mama and Toby cryin'? Do they have owies too?" Grandma, a real softie, wiped her eyes and took Ruby's hand and kissed it.

"Sometimes Mamas and Sisters have owies, honey, just like you."

"Can I see 'em?"

"No, honey, sometimes they are invisible? Like your friend Suzy who sometimes joins your tea parties."

"If you can't see 'em, how can you kiss 'em?" Ruby, never one to be motionless for long, jumped off Grandma's lap and hugged our legs. That broke the mushy mood, and we all ended up laughing.

"I believe you and Gary should try to find your dad. Bob and I have discussed everything and want to give you each $100 to help with the expenses because I know how expensive gas is.

You can take the Subaru; it's spacious and has air conditioning. Grandma will let me borrow her car if I need to. Grandma is also donating groceries. I'd feel more comfortable if you'd take Lena; she's a good watch dog, so we'll throw in a bag of kibble as well and the triple A card for emergencies."

"Woo-hoo! You guys are the best!" I ran to give both Mom and Grandma a hug.

"Me wanna hug too." How could I resist?

"Hey, Gary, with our money added to the cash from Mom and Bob, we'll actually be able to eat and maybe splurge on a motel for a shower and some TV."

"Okay, now that that's settled. I have a few requests." Gary and I looked at each other, expecting the worst. "Bob and I want you to check in with us every day, as many times as you need to." Then she paused. "And don't pick up hitchhikers."

"Thanks, Mom. You too, Grandma. We'll be careful, and I promise we won't pick up any hitchhikers. Do you still have Pops's St. Cloud address? We're planning to start there and then go to Ely and Grand Marais. After that, we'll see."

"Thank goodness for cell phones. I never thought I'd say that, and here I am a cheerleader for the darn things." Mom laughed. Mom resisted getting us cell phones. In fact, she refused to buy them, but Grandma stepped up to the plate and gave me one for my thirteenth birthday. A detective can't get along without a cell phone. And what's good for a sister is good for a brother, so Grandma felt she had to pop for Gary's as well.

At that point in our Hallmark Card moment, the front screen door slammed and Freddy joined us in the kitchen. Both Watson and Lena were so used to his barging in they didn't even bark. Sensitive boy that he is, he accurately assessed the emotional temperature of the room and decided it was safe. Then he sniffed the air.

"Are those sausages and patty cakes I smell?" Ruby started to clap her hands and sing.

"There's plenty to eat, Freddy. Join us."

"Do I have to play patty cake too?"

That was one of the best breakfasts I've ever had: good food, good conversation, and a happy family. Gary looked up at Mom and gave her a big thumb's up and a big goofy grin.

"Can I help clean up, Mrs. Murphy and Mrs. Tobias?" Freddy, always the gentleman, volunteered to clear the table. When he got up, he walked over to me and slipped me two twenties.

"Sis, I think our little road trip's a go. Get packin' and I'll meet you out back. We gotta a car to load."

"Remember what I said about that fake snake and the Foo Fighters."

"Yeah, yeah, I remember," he said, winking at Ruby who blinked back at him with both eyes.

Basilisk: A legendary reptile whose size and ugliness are reputed to be so powerful that a glance can turn you to stone. Just think Harry Potter.

Hallmark Card Moment: Hallmark cards and TV shows are sweet and cheesy. Everything turns out perfectly. A Hallmark moment, like our last breakfast before the road trip, was almost too good to be true. I happen to love Hallmark moments.

CHAPTER 10

Poop for the Poops

After talking to Mom and Grandma, we decided to wait until morning to leave for St. Cloud. I wanted to say good-bye to Bob and to thank him for his support and money. Plus, I wanted to double check that we had everything we needed. Mom found Pops's former address: 1317 8th Ave. North close to the St. Cloud Hospital. According to both the map and the computer it was Highway 94 all the way. Seventy-eight miles, about an hour and a half trip, depending on traffic. No problem.

Eight o'clock next morning came quickly. The family was gathered on the porch to say good-bye. It was going to be a hot one, in the high eighties with high humidity. My hair was already frizzing up into a red, wooly afro. I wore an old pair of cut offs and a tank top. I was dressing for comfort not fashion. Good thing there would be no cute boys on this trip. We loaded the car with the cooler, groceries, suitcases, map, cash, phones, Lena, and just as we were ready to get in the car, Mom said, "Kids, don't forget the sunscreen and the insect repellant." She ran from our front porch with Ruby on her hip. Ruby was holding the sunscreen.

"Toby, me squirt."

"Okay, Squirt, squirt." She sprayed stinky sunscreen on my arm.

"Ree, you too." She gave Gary a squirt. Since she first started to talk, Ruby called Gary "Ree." She couldn't say Gary, but she could say Toby. Go figure.

I could see this was going to be one of those long Minnesota good-byes. Gary looked at me and rolled his eyes. One last hug for everyone. "Remember, no hitchhikers no matter how cute. Love you, Toby. You too, Gary."

Just as we were pulling away from the curb, Freddy ran up to the open window, leaned down and kissed my cheek. "Good-bye, Toby. Good luck finding your dad. Call me, okay?"

"Thanks for everything, Freddy. Give Ole and Uber a hug for me." I wiped my eyes.

Wow, I wasn't expecting that. Gary, of course, teased me about having a boyfriend for about ten minutes and then became taciturn. I ignored him, lost in thought, until Albertville, the home of a very cool designer outlet mall and thirty six miles from St.Cloud.

"Gary, look, a cool outlet mall. Pleeese?" I whined.

He ignored me. No surprise there.

"Grandma would have stopped." I looked as the Banana Republic, Nike, and Gap signs swished past me which was a good thing I suppose because we couldn't afford to spend money on clothes or shoes. Oh, I hurt just thinking about it. The pain lasted until we got to the St. Cloud exit that also included information about getting to St. Cloud State University. Sure enough the same kid, who whizzed by the mall, found it in his stingy, female-hating heart to head on to the college.

"Gary, no fair!"

"Sis, since we're so close and since I've kinda been thinking of going to St. Cloud State, I figured it wouldn't cost any money just to look at the campus."

"Blah, blah, blah."

I stewed for a few minutes until I heard Lena whimper in the back seat. "I suppose Lena could use a little walk. Find a parking space and we'll snoop a little. I might get to meet a cool college dude."

"It's August, Sis, ain't going to happen." We pulled into a parking lot near Shoemaker Residence

Hall. I had just gotten out of the car with Lena on her leash, when this "kid" came up to us. He was about six feet four, thin, with long brown hair pulled back into a ponytail and he was carrying a camcorder and a backpack. He was wearing torn jeans and a T-shirt that said, *221-B Baker Street*. Be still my beating heart.

"Mind if I take some video of you and your handsome dog? What kind is she anyway?"

"Talkin' about my sister or the dog?" Gary piped in as he exited the driver's side, locking the car.

"Jacob Thomas Korkowski, wannabe film maker and photographer, at your service." Jacob took a formal little bow in my direction. "Most people call me J.T." He held out his hand to shake Gary's. I didn't know what to do so I curtsied to match his bow. He laughed. I blushed and so wished I wasn't having a bad hair day.

"I'm Gary and this is my sister, Toby. And, of course, Lena. Lena, shake."

J.T. bent down to shake her paw.

"Your dog's very handsome, the best thing I've seen on campus all day, present company excluded." I could feel my face getting hot.

"Lena is beautiful, I agree. Her mom was a good sized black lab and her dad was a standard sized white show poodle. Long story. I love her white markings. Ah, I like your T-shirt. I really really like mysteries, especially Sherlock Holmes..."

"Mind if I get some stills first?" It was like I was totally invisible, like he didn't hear anything I said.

He went into his backpack and took out a camera and screwed in a lens. Suddenly Lena became a different dog and started to pose. I swear she was showing off. She sat up straight and stared right at him, then cocked her head and perked up her ears. What a ham! The final pose was a beauty: she rolled on her back, pawed the air and seemed to say, "Please scratch my belly." Lena was turning into a dog-slut before my very eyes.

"She's a natural. Did you teach her this?"

"Are you kidding? She's just a normal pet. You know, we walk her, feed her, pick up her poop and that's about it," Gary said.

"You guys could make some money off her—take her to some commercial shoots; she's a natural."

"You go to school here?" Gary asked and J.T. nodded.

"I'm going to be a junior. Just finished summer school and wanted to take a break, you know, see some action, try to get some cool photos. Some guys and I rent a house close to campus. Livin' in the dorm gets to be real drag after awhile."

"Hey, J.T., could you show us around campus a bit? Gary's thinking of going here once he graduates, if he graduates."

"I've got my senior year under control, Sis. Just keep track of your own stuff, okay?" He flashed me a dirty look.

"Sure, I've got the time. I'm taking the bus 'up north' late this afternoon to check out a Blues Festival in Ely then I'll head down to St. Paul for the State Fair. I'm putting together a little film about good times in Minny. I'm trying to get my portfolio ready for my advanced filmmaking class next year. You can get some really great shots, people at their best, people at their worst. Sort of an artsy documentary, you know."

Gary looked at me, and I could almost hear his brain working. *We can save some money by having J.T. help with the gas and another guy to talk will save me going crazy with my little sister yapping about malls.*

"Funny thing, J.T., we're headed to Ely and some other places. Maybe you want to hang with us for awhile—help with some gas money?" I was standing behind J.T. and shaking my head at Gary, but he wasn't paying any attention. So much for bonding with my brother. So much for family time.

I had been deleted in less than five minutes by two men. At least I had Lena. Just then Lena leaned against J.T. and licked his hand. Make that deleted by two men and a dog.

"Sounds cool. I've got everything in my backpack. I keep it with me at all times because the equipment is kinda expensive, you know. Still want a tour?"

"Sure thing."

"Toby, do you mind if I walk Lena? She seems to like me."

Gary, J.T. and Lena walked and talked around the campus while I tagged along behind the "cool" kids, just like in junior high. I could hear Gary tell J.T. about our search for Pops. Every once in awhile I'd try to contribute to the conversation, but they talked over me. Typical boy behavior except for Freddy who actually knew how to listen.

The highlight of the walk was Lena's huge dump in front of the old Riverview building where all the English and foreign language classes were taught. I smiled and handed the boys two poop bags. Poop for the poops. Perfect.

Taciturn: A standard vocabulary word in those stupid state-wide assessments we have to take every year. It means quiet, non-talkative like Gary most of the time.

Camcorder: A digital hand-held camera and video recorder. J.T.'s most prized possession. He films and then it magically turns up on his computer. Go figure.

CHAPTER 11

All Will Be Well

After a quick picnic lunch in Munsinger Park across the river from the college, we headed out to where Pops supposedly lived for awhile.

With three years at St. Cloud State, (Go Huskies!), J.T. knew his way around the city. Good thing, too, because we were clueless.

I was trying to imagine Pops living here, going to work, buying groceries, making friends, living on 8th Avenue North and not in our old house in St. Paul. It kinda weirded me out, and it made me sad to think of all the time we'd lost together. Thank goodness I was in the back seat with Lena because I needed a hug and Lena was always up for a cuddle.

After about twenty minutes of touring the Granite City, we pulled up to this really cute chocolate brown house surrounded by a white picket fence. It was a cozy little story and a half with pots of red geraniums on the steps. We parked the Subaru right in front of the house, something that was kinda hard to do in our neighborhood. An older woman was puttering about in her yard, picking up sticks. After locking the car, we put Lena on her leash.

"Cute dog, kids," she said, walking through the gate. Everyone seemed to love our curly haired Lena. "Anything I can help you with?" She reached down to scratch Lena behind her ears.

"Actually, you could help us. We're trying to find our dad. We think he lived here for awhile about six years ago." Gary pulled out a photo of Pops. "Do you recognize him?"

The woman took the picture and studied it. Then she smiled. "That's Michael. He rented our basement apartment for about six months. Long time ago, but I remember him well. Nice guy. My late husband and I loved having him with us. He was clean, respectful, hard-working and paid his rent on time. The perfect tenant. My name is Betty Grundman, by the way. You can call me Betty."

We introduced ourselves.

"How about if I take Lena around the block while you guys talk?"

"Sounds like a plan. Thanks, J.T.," Gary said.

"What's the story on your dad, if you don't mind

my asking?" So Gary and I told her the abridged story, leaving out the accusation of embezzlement.

"Pops just left the marriage and us kids, but he did try to keep in touch through letters that our mother kept hidden from us. We found the letters a few days ago and now we're trying to find him and maybe get a few questions answered."

"Your mom and stepdad okay with this?" Betty asked.

"Actually they gave us their blessing and some cash to help fund the trip. They're cool with it," Gary said.

"Good. I wouldn't want you kids to be worrying your folks."

Just then J. T. came running from the end of the block, yelling Lena's name and holding her collar, ID tags dangling, and leash. He stopped at Betty's neighbor's to catch his breath, panting from the heat and exertion.

"Oh, my god, where's Lena?" I grabbed her collar and leash from J.T.. I wanted to grab him by his ponytail. Instead I got right up into his face and yelled, "What did you do to my dog?" I was ready to deck him.

"She got away, slipped out of her collar and went after a cat just a block away from here. I'm so sorry, Toby. She couldn't have gotten far."

"We're in St. Cloud, a strange city. She doesn't know where she is. And she doesn't have any identification. We've got to find her. Come on, Gary, let's go." I was pacing back and forth, feeling more and more panicky.

"Take a breath, Sis. Let's think this through. She's done this before and we've always found her."

"But that was at home. She's all alone and lost." I started to cry. Gary put his arm around me.

"Is she microchipped?" Betty asked.

"Yup, the people, who gave her to us, insisted."

"That's a huge plus. Most people know to take a lost dog to a vet. She obviously belongs to someone. Now show us where she disappeared, J.T."

"I'll get some dog food and a bottle of water just in case." I ran to the car.

"Good idea, Toby," Betty said. "I know the neighborhood and the neighbors. We'll find her, kids." And the four of us headed off in search of our beloved Lena.

Two hours later we returned to 1317 8th Ave. North alone. No dog. A few people said they saw a dog matching her description in the neighborhood, but the leads were dead ends.

Betty invited us in for something cool to drink and made a few phone calls to people she knew, including a local DJ who promised to make a few announcements on his show, but still no news of Lena. Gary and I couldn't relax, thinking of her out there by herself.

"You kids have to eat something. How about some sandwiches? After you cool off, you can head out again. It's nice to have the company."

"Betty, you've been so kind. First to Pops and then us." I started to cry again.

"I've got a few pictures of Lena. Why don't we take them to Kinkos and they can make up some lost dog flyers. Give me your cell phone number to put on the flyers. If it's okay with you, Betty, we can put your phone number on as well. We'll be right back. And then we can have those sandwiches."

"It's the least you can do. You're the one who lost the dog." I mumbled under my breath. Why did Gary insist J.T. come along? If he hadn't, we'd still have Lena.

"Why don't you help me with those sandwiches, Toby? If you would help set the table, that would be great. Then maybe you could give your folks a call and update them on the situation here. Tell them that you're welcome to stay the night. I can talk to them if you like." Betty was right. I needed to get in touch with Mom and Bob.

Once J.T. returned with twenty flyers, we had our supper and then continued to look for Lena until dark, pounding flyers into telephone poles and trees, but still no luck. Around 9:30 we gave J.T. a ride back to his house near campus. The plan was to get his college pals to help us look in the morning.

"What are we going to do if we don't find Lena tomorrow? Gary, what are we going to do? We can't just leave."

"I don't know, Toby. We might have to stay here a few days until we get Lena back. And we will get her back, Toby."

When we returned to Betty's, we said good night and thanked her, then headed for Pops's apartment. Between the heat and loosing Lena, I was knackered. I took a shower and got ready for bed.

The basement apartment wasn't half bad. It had a small living room with a couch for Gary, a small alcove with a single bed, a kitchenette and a three-quarters bath. I could almost imagine Pops living here. It was weird thinking that I would be sleeping in the same bed that he slept in for six months. It was oddly comforting. I felt like Pops was with me and telling me that "All will be well." Just like when I was a little girl. Whenever I was scared or hurt like when I broke my arm, he would hold me and tell me that everything would be okay, "All will be well, my sweet girl, all will be well." I fell asleep remembering how Pops sounded and how he smelled of aftershave.

Abridged: If you smushed all of the Harry Potter books into a single paperback, you'd have the abridged version. Get it?

Knackered: British slang for mostly dead.

Chapter 12

The Big Kahuna

About seven the next morning I heard someone knocking on the apartment door. I had been sleeping soundly, so it took me a few minutes to get oriented. Like I was in Pops's apartment in St. Cloud not in my room at home. Like Gary was snoring on the couch. Like Lena was lost. Like J.T. was bringing his college buddies to help find her. Like Betty was talking right outside the door. All those "likes" swarmed me like wasps to an open pop can.

"Toby, I've got some good news about Lena. A woman down the street found her and brought her in for the night. One of her kids saw a flyer. She couldn't wait any longer to call and I couldn't wait any longer to tell you. Sorry to wake you up so early. Great news, right?"

I opened the door to see Betty, her hair in pink spongy rollers, wearing a colorful *mumu*, and pink fluffy slippers, a vision of loveliness. *Not.* Then I looked at my own sleepwear: an oversized U of M T-shirt. My hair was totally in party mode and I hadn't been invited to the party. I wonder if those pink spongey curlers would help. Guess I shouldn't be so hasty to judge.

"You bet it's great news. I'll be right there as soon as I wake Gary, but he sleeps like the dead, so it might be awhile."

"No hurry, hon. I'll be upstairs making us some breakfast. Do you kids like pancakes?"

"Love 'em. Thanks, Betty." Just thinking of patty cakes made me homesick.

"Gary, wake up." He was snorting and puffing away. He sounded just like Pops. One time Pops fell asleep on the porch swing and snored so loudly that all the neighborhood kids gathered around and pointed and laughed until Grandma shooed them away. Must be genetic—goofy male chromosomes and all that. I'm far too feminine to sound like a Harley.

"Bro, get your sorry butt outta bed." *Nada.* I shook him, I tickled his feet, I took the snake that I knew he had hidden in his duffel bag and dangled it in front of his face. Nothing worked until I tried what Mom called "Mommy's special wake-up call."

We called it "Mommy water boarding." Let me explain.

After she poured ice water in a spray bottle, she'd stand over her sleeping victim, that'd be Gary, and spray the ice cold water on his face. The victim's first response was to wipe it away and continue snoring. Then Mommy Dearest would open the spray bottle and pour a little of the icy liquid on said victim. If the person's mouth was open, she would pour just a little in the open mouth.

Usually the victim emerged from dreamland sputtering, spitting, and furious. She only had to use it once on me and I learned my lesson, but Gary experienced Mom's tough love on many occasions.

"Gary, last chance to avoid Sissy's special wake-up call." Since I didn't have a spray bottle handy, I went directly to the fridge and got some ice from the freezer, a glass, and some water. Shazam! I was already at step two: Pour ice cold water on victim.

"What the...!" Gary sat up, with his hair all spiked and the slippery, wet snake stuck to his chest.

"Gotcha!" By this time I was really laughing. Gary not so much.

"I get to use the bathroom first. By the way, Betty just said a neighbor called and has Lena! Looks like we'll be on our way after breakfast. You'll need to call J.T." I scooted to the bathroom while Gary grumbled something about revenge. He threw the snake at the bathroom door.

After packing we joined Betty in the dining room. There we found the table set beautifully with fresh flowers, cloth napkins, a bowl of fresh fruit, and a pitcher of orange juice—the whole shebang!

"Wow, this is awesome!" Gary said as he sat down and helped himself to some fruit.

"It's a pleasure to cook for someone. I usually just have cereal and coffee for breakfast," Betty said. "Anyone want coffee besides me?"

I have never acquired a taste for coffee unlike Gary who went through coffee like Patty Washington did boyfriends.

We had a leisurely breakfast, considering I wanted my pooch back. But I also figured we needed to grill Betty on Pops and where he might be. We might not have another chance.

"That was super nummy, Betty. Thank you so much. Last night we were so focused on Lena that we didn't have a chance to ask you any more questions. Are you up for some interrogating?"

"Sure thing, kids. I'll try to help you find Michael. I knew he had kids because he talked about you both all the time, but I didn't want to pry. How did you end up here, by the way?"

"Pops mentioned granite quarries in one of his letters and, well, St. Cloud is Granite City. Then when we confronted Mom about the letters, she told us your address. It was the only sure thing we had," I said.

"We've got some more clues from the letters: Boundary Waters, wolves, camping, lake snow effect. Can you think of any more, Toby?"

"Dog sledding and there was something about a hospital. I'd have to get the letters to be sure."

"Well, that makes sense because your dad mentioned something about a friend in Ely who was going to help him find a job. Ely fits. And there is an international center for wolves up there."

"Gary, we were right about Ely. We need to talk to Mom. Maybe she knows who these Ely friends are. And we need to tell her about Lena, so she doesn't worry. Just a few more questions if that's okay."

Betty told us he was driving an old truck with a pop-up camper attached so he'd never be "homeless." And he worked at McDonald's. Wow! Pops slinging burgers and driving an old truck. Go figure.

"I'll call J.T. to tell him he doesn't need to rally the troops. The pooch has been found," Gary said as he pulled out his phone.

"Can I help you clean up, Betty?"

"No, you kids have more important things to do like make phone calls. I can handle it. Thanks anyway."

Mom told us about a college roommate who was a native Elyian or Elyiat, er, resident of Ely. That just might be the Big *Kahuna* of leads. But first we had to get our girl, Lena.

Mumu: A loose fitting dress that covers up a multitude of figure faults. I didn't want to imagine what faults Betty was hiding.

Waterboarding: A form of torture where a cloth is put over the face and then water is poured so that the victim feels like he is drowning. Mom skipped the cloth.

Mommy Dearest: Joan Crawford, a famous dead actress, was supposedly abusive to her daughter, Christina. So Christina wrote a memoir called *Mommy Dearest* and made tons of money. Everyone likes reading about dirty little secrets. Hmm ...maybe I should write a memoir?

The Big *Kahuna:* Hawaiian word that means "big shot." Finding out Pops had friends in Ely might be the clue, the "big shot" of clues, that will lead us to our Pops.

CHAPTER 13

Itchin' to Find Pops

By the time we had loaded the car, hugged and thanked Betty a gazillion times, we were ready to pick up our tagalong buddy, J.T., and then retrieve Lena. When Gary talked to J.T., he insisted that he film the reunion even though we would have to backtrack to the south side of town. J.T. loved the story of *Finding Pops* so much that he wanted to film the whole thing and make a movie about us. He was willing to dump the Ely Blues Festival and the State Fair to film a human interest story. We were going to be movie stars! Wait 'til Freddy gets a load of that! If I'd only known, I would have brought nicer clothes and some makeup.

Heading back to the north side of St. Cloud to pick up our beloved pooch, we stopped at a florist's along the way and bought a beautiful bouquet of flowers for Lena's rescuers, heavy on the daisies because they were cheap,. And we also stopped at a convenience store for more ice and beverages. We still had plenty of food.

As we got closer to Betty's neighborhood, J. T. started filming out the car window. In fact, he never stopped filming. When we got to "Lena's house" only two blocks from Betty's, the front screen door was open, and we could hear squeals and squeaks from Lena who was all wiggles and curls. We could see her jumping up and down like a Pogo Stick.

We knocked on the door, and this cute little boy about four opened the door and let out our wild and crazy pup who engulfed us with licks and leaps. Talk about a happy dog. Then I looked at the little boy's face and he was crying. His mom picked him up, and he buried his face in her shoulder.

"Sam just loved Lena. They slept together; he was so hoping you wouldn't come to get her and that Lena could be his dog. I'm Carrie, by the way."

"I'm so sorry, Sam, but you know what?" Sam stopped crying and looked at me. "J.T. took lots of pictures of Lena, and if your mommy would give us your address, we'll send you an autographed picture of Lena. We'll get her to put her paw print on the photo."

I gently poked Sam in his tummy like I did to Ruby. He giggled.

"Lena and you and your mommy are going to be

in a movie J.T. is making about us. We'll tell you all about it. Thank you so much for rescuing her."

Carrie put Sam down and he ran to give Lena a good-bye hug.

"These are for you." I handed her the bouquet, picking out a daisy to give to Sam. "Thanks again." Sam took the daisy, smiled shyly and wiped his eyes.

After exchanging names and addresses, we headed back to the south side where we picked up MN 23 E and then on to I-35 N to Ely, about 240 miles north, a four to five hour drive depending on traffic and any surprises we may encounter. There always seemed to be plenty of those.

As we were nearing Duluth, I said to Gary, "Why don't we find a spot for a picnic and maybe even a swim. There are lots of lakes around here, and Lena would love to go for a walk and cool dip. What do ya think, Bro? J.T.?"

At hearing her name, Lena woke up and whined. So did J.T. wake up, that is. Big surprise that he had an opinion.

"Let's get a little north of Duluth, Gary. I remember swimming in Pike Lake at a public beach in Canosia Township when I was a kid. We could take a break and picnic there. Check your map, Toby."

"Sure thing, Boss." I said, mimicking Freddy. I really missed Freddy. J.T. really missed the sarcasm.

After a few minutes fumbling with my Minnesota map, I found Pike Lake. We were there in less than an hour.

We pulled up to the public beach and were surprised there were so few people there, considering the heat wave. I was wearing cut offs, but didn't have a suit. The guys were wearing shorts. No suits there either. All I wanted to do was wade in some cool water with my pooch.

"Let's cool off first and then eat," I suggested. Since there were so few people and no dogs, we let Lena off leash and boy, was she happy. I waded in the water along with Gary and it felt awesome. Having rolled up my cut offs to very short shorts, I could get wet without getting my clothes soaked. It was perfect. While Gary and I were romping, J.T. was filming away with Lena by his side. She wouldn't come near the water. Go figure.

"Put down that camera and join us," I yelled at J.T.

"No way, I'm having way too much fun watching and filming you two."

We stayed in the cool water for about fifteen minutes and joined J.T. at the picnic area. It was then we noticed the sign: *Beaches closed due to swimmer's itch.* So that's why the beach was nearly empty; we should have known something was going on. Duh.

"Did you see the sign, J.T.? Is that why you didn't join us?" If he had seen the warning and didn't say anything, he was in deep doo-doo.

"Nah, I saw it the same time you did. Besides swimmer's itch isn't so bad. These little microscopic parasites burrow under your skin, and you itch like crazy for a few days. You just use calamine lotion and the itching goes away." So speaketh The Expert.

"What happens to the parasites?"

"They just get full and leave. Just joshin' ya, Toby. Actually, they don't like people and die. We'll get some calamine once we get to Ely. You'll be fine."

"Easy for you to say," Gary said. Maybe this guy bonding thing was getting old. I could only hope.

By late afternoon both Gary and I had a red, itchy rash all over our legs. It freaked me out thinking of the bugs burrowing under my skin. Eww. Fortunately, we didn't have our suits or we'd have been red and rashy all over. Double Eww. Once we applied the calamine lotion, the itching lessened a lot. Only thing was we looked like someone pink-washed us. A great look for a budding film star and private eye! Good thing Leaping Lena stayed with J.T. 'cause I wouldn't want to have to take her to a vet.

When we called Mom back at Betty's to check in, she gave us the name of Pops's college roommate, Luca Cadenza, who grew up in Ely. While we were still at Betty's, I used her computer and checked him out. Sure enough, he still lived in Ely. And he ran an Italian restaurant. Lucky for us he was a restauranteur and not a hit man for the Italian Mafia.

We pulled up to Luca's Italian Ristorante around four—before the blue hairs came out for the Early Bird Specials. Luca's brown stucco exterior was brightened by red and white striped awnings and window boxes filled with red geraniums and a vine that Mom used in her window boxes at home. There were tables and chairs on the sidewalk so that diners could experience the best of alfresco dining. Although Ely wasn't exactly what I'd call picturesque, there was a sweet little park across the street.

"Gary, what are we going to do with Lena? It's way too hot to keep her in the car."

"I'll take her over to the park. We can wait for you in the shade while you check out this lead."

"Hang on to her this time, will you?" I was still kind of freaked about Lena's escape in St. Cloud.

"Got it."

"Thanks, J.T."

We opened the doors to a blast of air-conditioning which felt absolutely wonderful. I hoped it was dark enough to camouflage my pink legs.

"Sorry kids, we're not open yet for dinner," said the hostess with the mostest. At least in the boob department. She was seriously gifted, so much so that Gary's eyes bugged out, and I swear I saw some drool dripping from his mouth. Then she looked at my legs and at Gary's. So much for lack-of-light camouflage.

"You kids must have missed the sign up at Pike Lake. That looks like some serious swimmer's itch. Bummer. What can I do for you?" she asked, batting her mascara coated eyelashes. She looked like she'd been held upside down and dipped in a vat of Cover Girl medium beige.

"My name's Gary Martin. This is my sister, Toby. You see, Toby and I—we're trying to find our father and we thought he might have stayed here in Ely for a while," Gary said. "His college roommate was Luca Cadenza."

Shazam! Magic word: Luca Cadenza. Her face softened. "Swimmer's itch and a search for Papa.

How can I resist? Have a seat and I'll get you a few sodas. And I'll get Luca. My name's Sherry, by the way." She led us to a booth covered in maroon faux leather with duct tape covering the cracks. The table was covered in a red checked table cloth with a Chianti bottle acting as a candle holder. Very classy. *Not.*

"Man, did you see those hooters? Lucky Luca."

"Give it a rest, college boy wannabe. She's a sweet older lady." I felt obligated to defend our waitress/hostess/pole dancer because she gave us free sodas and had a nice smile.

A few minutes later she came with our beverages and a short, squat Italian man who I assumed was Luca. He sported long hair that curled at his collar and a four o'clock shadow. Wearing a simple white shirt and jeans, he looked totally harmless, unlike Luca Brasi from *The Godfather*. He sat down opposite me and Gary.

"So kids, what do you want to know about Michael? I see you've met my personal trainer, Sherry Trifle." He grinned at Sherry and gave her a little wink and a pat on the butt.

Person trainer. Right. More like exotic dancer turned restaurant hostess turned girlfriend.

After about five minutes of interviewing Luca, we found out that Pops had spent a few weeks in Ely.

"Do you have any idea where he might have gone?" I asked, getting frustrated at what seemed to be a dead end. I started to scratch.

"You mentioned some letters, right? If it's not my business, just say so, but I might be able to see with fresh eyes, ya know?"

"Mr. Cadenza, we brought our dog and a friend along with us and they're out in the park across the street. Can we...?"

"Bring 'em in. Sure thing. We can't have them suffering out there in the heat and humidity. We have an air-conditioned back storage room where we can give the dog some water and let him relax while we talk."

"Lena's a girl. Thanks, Mr. Cadenza. I'll tell them and then get the letters from the car. Be right back."

I heard him say as I was leaving, "Sherry, order these kids one of Luca's special pizzas on the house." Just hearing the word *pizza* made my mouth water. Now *pizza*—there's a magic word.

When I was walking back to the restaurant, I noticed two flyers taped on Luca's windows, advertising a presentation for tonight by Ursula Grauler on the "Bears of Ely." Bears and swimmer's itch—nice place, Ely.

Blue hairs: Have you seen these seriously old ladies fresh from the hairdressers? They have their hair colored, but sometimes the dye turns their hair blue-gray. Bob calls old ladies "blue hairs" or "cue tips" depending on hair color. I get why Grandma dyes her hair red.

Alfresco: This is just the fancy way to describe eating outside. Those Italians, you know.

Faux: French for fake like in fake leather or fur. Some of the snooty-patooties at my school are totally *faux*.

Luca Brasi: Luca was the Godfather's main hit man in Mario Puzo's novel of the same name. He was one scary dude.

CHAPTER 14

In the Pink

When I got Lena settled in the cool storage room with water, some kibble, and her favorite squeaky toy, I joined Gary and J.T. at our table. Luca was entertaining the guys with a few lame Italian jokes: "If Tarzan and Jane were Italian, what would Cheetah be?" Pause. "The least hairy of the three." An explosion of laughter.

"Did I mention my sister is Italian?" J.T. covered a laugh with a cough and Luca had the good sense not to even crack a smile, so Gary found himself laughing by himself.

"Did I mention my brother is a jerk?" I looked down at my hairy legs and realized I needed a shave. Thank goodness for the calamine.

I handed Luca the packet of letters. "I'll just read them at the bar where it's quiet."

Just then Sherry delivered our Luca's Special Deluxe Pizza covered with pepperoni, sausage, peppers, olives, onions, fresh tomatoes, and tons of cheese. The crust was thin, crisp and easy to pick up. That being said, I managed to drip cheese down the front of my T-shirt and accessorize with red sauce. With my pink calamine-lotioned legs and my Italian Special Deluxe T-shirt, I looked like a hippy flamingo.

After J.T. had a few pieces, he started filming once again, including a close up of the strings of mozzarella hanging from my chin. And from Gary's. At least Gary was looking equally disgusting. *Noshing with the Martins*—a new reality show perhaps. After about fifteen minutes of gobbling the best pizza ever, I couldn't wait any longer and walked over to the bar.

"So what do ya think, Mr. Cadenza? Any idea where Pops might have gone?"

"That I do, young lady. I'll be right over." He filled his glass with draft beer and joined us.

As soon as he sat down, we started questioning him.

"Did he stay here for awhile?" Gary asked.

"A couple of weeks, like I said. While he was here, I tried to find him some work, but the jobs were pretty limited."

"Did he ever mention us?"

"Yes, he did, Toby. He was quite proud of both

of you, but whenever he talked about you guys, he seemed nervous and edgy. When I asked him about it, he was evasive. Now I know why."

"He was exonerated, by the way," I said.

"Glad to hear it. Michael left after about two weeks, and I think I may have some ideas about where he might have gone." We all sat up straighter.

"Don't keep us in suspense," I said, scratching my leg. I needed more calamine lotion and soon.

"Some words and phrases caught my eye when I was reading the letters: *apples, Madeline, Mission Hill.*"

"We noticed the same words, but didn't have a clue about what they meant," Gary said.

"When Sherry and I were on vacation last October, we went to Bayfield, WI during their very famous apple festival. Amazing. I've never eaten so many apple fritters, doughnuts, pies, breads, jams, jellies, you name it. They even had apple flavored mustard." I rolled my eyes. Mustard—who cares? I wanted more info on Pops.

"Then we took the ferry to Madeline Island."

"Wow! Madeline was referring to an island and not a woman's name. We thought maybe Pops found himself a lady friend," Gary said. All the time J.T. was filming away.

"Anything else?" I asked, wanting to believe that Luca had solved the mystery.

"While we were walking around the island, we stopped for coffee at the Mission Hills Coffee Shop where the coffee and apple crisp were delicious, by the way. And I seem to remember that the owners' names were Jim and Marie, at least that's what the menu said."

"Woo-hoo! It all fits! High fives all around." I slapped hands with the boys. "Now we just need to drive to Bayfield and hope Pops is still there. Let's go, Bro." I got up to leave. The guys followed.

"Hold your horses, kids, you can't head out tonight; it's over 200 miles away and you shouldn't be driving that far in the dark with the wolves and bears out there. Why don't you stay with Sherry and me for the night, give a call to your folks, and get a fresh start in the morning? We're headed out to the lecture after the dinner rush if anyone's interested."

"What will we do with Lena?" I asked.

"No problem. She'll bunk with you. Sherry and I both love animals. How is she with cats?"

"She's real friendly and won't cause any trouble, I promise." I noticed Gary scratching his legs and shaking his head. A real multi-tasker, my brother.

"Just let me know your plans. We live above the

restaurant so you don't have to do any more driving tonight. Sherry can scoot upstairs to get the bedroom ready—clean sheets and all that. You know how women are. Plus, she'll want to meet the pooch."

As soon as Luca left, Gary looked at me. "'She's real friendly,'" he said mimicking me. "Has Lena even been around cats? What if she eats their cat?"

"What if the cat's aggressive? I saw this cat attack a bear on You Tube. Lena might be the one who gets hurt."

"Guess I'd better be ready to film the excitement. You guys are great subject material for a movie."

"Let's get the layout of the apartment and see if Lena could be confined to one of our rooms. We can also meet the cat. I hope there's only one," Gary said. "Are we all in agreement we're going to spend the night here?"

I looked at J.T., and he gave me a thumb's up. "Guess it's a go."

After we told Mr. Cadenza and Sherry our plans, we headed to the car for our gear and then on to Laura Ashley hell, aka Luca and Sherry's flat.

Imagine pink, rose, lavender, and white flowers exploding over walls, floors, furniture, even the kitchen ceiling fan. Lacy white curtains covered all the windows. Don't get me started on the fringy lampshades or the fake ferns, the silk flower arrangements, and the ceramic bunnies. The living room couch was rose velvet with chairs in a floral satinlike fabric; all in all I felt nauseous. Sherry took the shabby chic cottage look to a whole new level. How could Mr. Cadenza stand being in this estrogen explosion, this floral barf?

With all that pink, Gary and I fit in well with our calomined legs. No sign of a real cat anywhere, though I did see a huge stuffed white cat on Luca and Sherry's bed. There were two things in the apartment's favor: the air-conditioning and the free lodging. Anything was better than sleeping in the car with two boys and a dog.

The boys shared the lavender guest room with Lena and I claimed the rose velvet couch. Lucky me.

"Now that you're all clean, are you kids up for a little educational lecture?" Sherry asked. She was dressed in (surprise surprise!) a floral print sundress.

"Can I go in shorts 'cause I didn't bring any dress up clothes?"

"Do you want to wear something of mine?" *I'd rather shoot myself.*

"Shorts are just fine. Things are pretty casual in Ely," Luca added.

"Thanks, Sherry, but I'm okay in my shorts. Guys, are you coming along to learn about the 'Bears in Ely,' a lecture given by Ms. Ursula Grauler Ph.D.?"

"Ursula, isn't that Latin for bear?" J.T., Mr. College Kid, said.

"And don't bears growl? What a great name for a bear-whisperer," I said.

"I'm in just because of her name. There's got to be a cool story that goes with that name," Gary said. J.T. decided to stay in Sherry's Floral Boutique to watch TV. He promised to walk Lena one more time before we turned in. Still no sign of a cat.

That night's lecture turned out to be one of the most helpful and practical of my life.

Nosh: Yiddish for nibble only we weren't nibbling; we were devouring the pizza.

Trifle: A British dessert of cake, custard, whipped cream, jam, and sherry. Sherry's parents must have been dessert-fiends or else that was Sherry's "stage" name.

Laura Ashley: A Welsh fashion designer who created girly girl fabric patterns with lots of flowers. The inspiration for the Sherry Trifle Flower Barf.

Flat: That's Brit talk for apartment. Maybe Gary's right; maybe I do watch too much PBS.

CHAPTER 15

Is the Bear a Catholic?

All night I dreamed I was being chased by creatures with purple velvet flower heads and creepy, crawly, viney fingers that wrapped around my throat. And the flowers growled ferociously with bared teeth and smelly breath. When I woke up, I saw a huge, white, long-haired cat sleeping on my chest and making noise like a motor boat. "What the ...?" When he heard me, he looked at me with utter disdain and jumped down with a thud.

"I see you've met Snowball," Sherry said. "He's rather shy, but he seems to fancy you." As soon as he heard his name, Snowball waddled to his mistress, expecting some sort of smelly treat, no doubt. The stuffed cat on Luca and Sherry's bed was Snowball! Go figure. I was slowly waking up. Man, what a rough night.

"That's my baby," Sherry said, picking up the hairy lump. "I named him after the white hydrangeas that I love so much. People used to call them snowballs."

Sherry named her cat after a flower? That girl was just full of surprises.

"Sorry to wake you and Snowball up, but the boys were eager to get going. They've already had cereal and walked and fed Lena. They're outside waiting. You were sound asleep. I'm surprised you didn't hear them."

I was being suffocated by Snowball, that's why.

"Can I fix you some breakfast?"

"No thanks. I'm not all that hungry. Guess I ate too much pizza last night. You and Luca have been great. Thanks for everything." I used the bathroom, brushed my teeth, washed my face, wore all the same clothes I slept in, and was good to go.

Even though Luca and Sherry were generous, I couldn't wait to get on the road. Except for my stuff, the guys had loaded the car; apparently they felt the same way. The morning was cool, almost fall-like, and considerably less humid; Lena had her head out the window and barked when she saw me. I was ready to find Pops. On to Duluth, US Hwy 53 South and then WI 13 South to

Bayfield—about 200 miles or four hours, not counting any stops for gas, food or dog walks.

A few miles outside of Virginia I felt an uncomfortable rumbling in my belly, never a good sign when you're traveling. Maybe I was just hungry, but I was getting increasingly uncomfortable.

"Gary, I need you to stop so I can go to the bathroom."

"We're in the middle of nowhere, Toby. You'll to wait until we get to Duluth."

"I can't wait, Gary. I mean it." The cramps were increasing in intensity. I started to rummage through Grandma's bag of groceries for some tissue or paper towels. *Paper towels will have to work.*

"I need you to pull over NOW, Gary. J.T., if you film this you're dead."

Gary pulled over to the side of the road. I ran down into the ditch and off into the woods, not wanting the boys to see me. I could hear them laughing as I dashed off. I looked back to see J.T. filming every minute. What a turd.

Great, just great, I'm in the woods taking a crap and everybody will know it because that little creep is filming. And soon my bodily functions will be in a film and I will be fecally famous. Reese Witherspoon could play me.

I walked a little deeper, the trees providing a leafy canopy. The sun sneaked through the trees, casting shadows everywhere. If I hadn't been in considerable discomfort, I would have enjoyed the solitude and the beauty much more.

Hoping that I wasn't squatting in poison ivy, I did what I had to do. It was beautiful here: quiet, with the exception of the birds, and very peaceful, now that the cramps subsided. I might have to stay here forever just to avoid facing the public ie. two jerky boys, one with an annoying camcorder.

When I was about ready to use the paper towels, I heard some noise: twigs breaking and leaves rustling. Someone was out there! Ohmigod, I was going to be killed by a Mesabi monster. Then I heard heavy breathing. A perverted Mesabi monster. I did the quickest wipe ever, pulled up my pants, turned around, ready to fight for my life and looked right at a huge black bear about fifty feet away.

What did Ursula say last night? Come on, Toby, think. You can do this. Remember what she said about encountering a bear in the wild. Stay calm. Right, that was the first rule. Oh, yeah, back away slowly, but don't turn your back on him. That's number two. I can do that. I just did a big number two.

I walked slowly and calmly backwards right into a tree. I yelled, "Sh*t!" *That's right, make noise, Toby. Make a lot of noise; Oh, yeah, that's rule number three.* "Go back home, Bear!" I yelled, waving my arms. He grunted and rose up on his hind legs.

Okay, Bear, maybe I need a more gentle approach; I need to go back to number one.

"Hi Bear. It's Toby, Bear, your new best friend." I said with a shaky voice. That was sorta what Ursula said to her bears. The bear looked at me like he understood what I was saying. And then he growled, a big black bear growl.

Now I remembered number four: *Do not run.* Then I did exactly what I wasn't supposed to do: I turned my back on him and got the hell outta Dodge. The hell with number two and number four!

Fortunately, I wasn't too far from the road. Stumbling madly through the brush, I got to the ditch with the bear lumbering and snorting behind me. I yelled at the boys to open the car door and start the car. I could hear Lena barking her head off. Just as I got to the car, the bear scrambled up the ditch, looked at us and stood up on his hind legs and let out an enormous growl.

I was gasping for breath. As soon as I knew I was safe about two blocks away, I started to shake and hugged Lena. I looked back and saw the bear amble across the road like our encounter was no big deal.

"Holy crap, I got all of that on camera! That was incredible!"

"So glad I could accommodate your creative needs." He was beginning to really irritate me.

"You okay, Sis?"

"I think so," I said, snuggling Lena. "Other than almost becoming bear food, I'm just peachy. So glad I provided such exciting footage, J.T., you insensitive clod."

Then I noticed Lena had a large scratch on her nose which I examined carefully. "Either of you guys know how Lena got the scratch?"

"Lena got a little up close and personal for Snowball's taste. That cat has a mean right cross," J.T. said, laughing.

Now he was really getting under my skin.

I could only imagine what my face would have looked like if I had gotten a little too "up close and personal" with Mr. Bear.

By this time, I was starting to get my *mojo* back. I was royally pissed, especially at J.T. The bear and Snowball not so much.

We rode in total silence for the next half hour. Then out of the blue J. T. started to sing:

"The Grizzly Bear is huge and wild;
He has devoured the infant child.

The infant child is not aware
It has been eaten by a bear."

"Not bad singing for an 'insensitive clod,'" Gary said. "Only it wasn't a grizzly bear. It was a black bear and they aren't as aggressive."

"Easy for you to say, Bro; you weren't looking at him up-close and personal. Where did you get that song, J.T.?"

"It's from a poem by A. E. Housman. My dad used to sing it to me when I was a kid. Then he'd pretend he was bear and try to eat me. It always turned into a wrestling match where I'd end up in a bear hold."

"Is your dad still around?" I was curious.

"Nah, he died of cancer when I was twelve." Maybe that was why J.T. was so interested in our search for Pops.

"Sorry, J.T." I felt bad that I'd called him 'insensitive.'

Another twenty minutes of silence. I was thinking about Grandma, about how we could have lost her.

"How about we stop in Superior for some lunch? My treat. I'm sick of eating out of the cooler," I said, breaking the silence. "We can park in the shade and leave the windows open for Lena."

"Sounds great, Toby. Maybe we'll get lucky and find a Culver's. I could really go for a Butter Burger with the works, some onion rings, and a Cement Mixer."

"Me too."

"Me three."

As we were getting out of the car in the Culver's parking lot, Gary said, " Does a detective sh*t in the woods?"

I answered, "Is the bear a Catholic?"

"Hot damn, that girl is quick." J.T. grinned and gave me a thumb's up.

Old joke alert: In the old days, folks would say about something obvious: "Is the Pope a Catholic? Does a bear sh*t in the woods?" This was one of Grandma's favorites; Gary and I just changed it up a bit.

Mesabi: One of four iron ore mines known as the Iron Range, home of the Mesabi monster or The Bear

Arthur Edward Houseman aka A. E. Houseman: An old British poet (March 26, 1859 — April 30 1936) who wrote this poem that eventually turned into a drinking song. I could have used a drink after my encounter with the bear.

CHAPTER 16

Mooningwanekaaning

Cool weather, sunshine, blue skies, white fluffy clouds, colorful sailboats, and Lake Superior. Beautiful. I could get used to this. We walked the little town of Bayfield, looking at the Victorian cottages, the signs for fish boils, the wild and crazy Maggie's Cafe decorated with pink flamingos. We showed Pops's picture to as many businesses as we could in a few hours, but no "hits." So we decided to take the ferry over to Madeline Island, the "gateway to the Apostle Islands," according to the tourist center brochure.

We were just in time for the 4:30 ferry to the island. We drove the car onto the ferry, which was kinda weird. A really cute guy showed us where to park. We all wanted to see everything, so we got out and went to the upper level. Lena was allowed as long as she was leashed. The water, the rocky shoreline, the sailboats were breathtakingly beautiful. I felt like I was on an ocean somewhere, maybe in Italy or France. Lena put her face to the wind and I could swear she was grinning. We all were. Even if we didn't find Pops, we'd had a wonderful road trip. I was even getting to like J.T., not like *like*, like I like Freddy, but like as a friend. How was that for the "like" record, Mrs. Trattles?

Our plan was to find the Mission Hills Coffee Shop, our best lead. Since it was the only coffee shop on the island, it was easy to find. J.T. kept Lena on a leash outside while Gary and I went inside. The coffee shop was small with only a few tables. The display cases were cluttered with faded T-shirts and silly toys for sale, the usual souvenir junk, but I could smell brownies. Always an excellent sign. We had to stand in line for a few minutes before an older lady took our order.

"May I help you, young lady?"

"I hope so." I pulled Pops's picture from my pocket and showed it to her. Suddenly her face lit up into the biggest grin.

"Are you Toby, Michael's daughter?" I nodded. "I thought I recognized the red hair." Then she looked at Gary, "And you must be Gary."

Talk about being gobsmacked! She knew us, so she must have known Pops. And Pops must have shown her pictures of us.

"Jim, could you man the register while I talk to Michael's kids? Grab some brownies for the kids while you're at it."

"Michael's kids, you gotta be joshin'. How did they get here?"

"If you'd get over here, I might find out the answer to that question."

"I'm going to give Michael a call; I'll be just a few minutes."

"No problem. Sorry, kids, I've got to stay here for a few minutes while Jim talks to your dad. Make yourselves comfortable."

A few minutes later Jim returned. "Your dad said to show you around the gallery and take you to his cabin. He said he'd stop by Maggie's for takeout and to help yourself to anything in the fridge if you're hungry. Until then try some of Marie's famous brownies." He handed me a plate of pure decadence.

"Thanks, hon. Come on, kids, let's go into the back room to talk. It's only open to the public when Michael is going to have a show. Lucky you, he's having one this coming weekend."

We had found Pops. The Pops we knew was an accountant and the Pops we found was an artist.

"Oh, my god, look at this," I said when I walked into the room. Instead of the schlocky touristy souvenirs in the main room, there were beautiful, colorful, Dr. Seussian bird houses in the shapes of outhouses, high rises, cabins, chalets; you name it, there they were. I bet there were fifty or more in shades of orange, yellow, pink, blue, green. hanging on the walls and sitting on shelves.

A rainbow of birdhouses that curved, swayed, and danced. It was a birdhouse museum. There were other artsy items as well: painted chairs, tables, even lamps, all with a whimsical Dr. Seuss feeling to them. I could imagine all of these items in Whoville. I was in love.

"J.T., are you getting all this?"

"Almost better than the bear, Toby. I'll do a quick survey of the art, then I'll take Lena for a walk, if that's okay."

"Thanks, J.T.," Gary said.

"They're wonderful, aren't they? Michael has made quite the name for himself as an artist; once people see these, they're hooked. We have many repeat customers; he keeps very busy. He even sells in the Twin Cities."

So that's how the letters got mailed. That question was answered.

"Where is he now? When can we see him?" Gary was finally regaining speech.

"He should be back from Duluth early this

evening. He took a load of houses to a gallery in Canal Park. How long's it been since you've seen him?"

"Over six years, but he did write. The thing is: We just got the letters a few days ago. Our mom kept them from us," I said.

"So how did you end up here?" Marie asked.

"We read and re-read the letters. Grandma and a friend helped us figure out some of the references. To make a long story short, the letters led us to St. Cloud where he stayed and worked, then to Ely, also referenced in the letters. Mom told us about an old college friend who lived in Ely and he recognized the references to Madeline Island. We thought Madeline might be Pops's girlfriend." Marie laughed at that.

"One of the letters mentioned woodworking, but we had no idea," Gary said, as if waking up from a dream.

"No one did. I think even he was surprised at the reaction to his art. It was about five years ago when Michael showed up in his old camper, looking for work. It was our busy season, so we took him on for a few months in the shop here. He rented out our garage and used it for a workshop. When he showed us some of his birdhouses, we insisted he display them in the shop. They lasted a few hours.

The more he made, the more he sold. Soon he couldn't keep up with the tourist demands. Once he took some to galleries in Bayfield and Duluth, the word was out. The rest, they say, is history."

"So now he lives here permanently? Even in the winter?"

"Well, that's when he does most of his work. We decided to rent this back room to him in the winter when it was too cold to camp. He worked in the heated garage, slept in this room, cooked his meals in the kitchen. It helped us, too, having someone here, watching over things. Once he started making a decent living, he bought the cabin and worked on that."

"How do you get supplies and stuff?"

"The ferries usually run through mid-January unless we have unusually cold weather and the lake freezes over; then we have wind sleds that take us across. We try to plan carefully and stock up on supplies. Living on an island is not for the faint of heart."

I kept walking around looking at Pops's art. I imagined what Ruby, Mom, and Grandma would say if they could see them. Maybe I had enough money to buy one of the small birdhouses for each of them. Then I checked the price tag of the smallest house. Holy moly guacamole! Even with a family discount I couldn't afford even one.

"Well, kids, ready to check out your dad's digs?"

"Sure thing. It's Marie isn't it? Pops mentioned you and Jim in one of his letters."

"Sometimes I think I've misplaced my brain. I should have introduced myself right away."

"I understand; we did surprise you. Our friend is waiting outside with our dog. Will Pops mind if we bring Lena to his house?"

"No, he loves animals and has two cats of his own. Question is: Will the cats mind?"

"She's real friendly and won't cause any trouble, I promise," Gary said, quoting me.

"Good, 'cause Michael's real fond of those kitties. I think you're in for a pleasant surprise when you see your dad's place," Marie said as we went out to retrieve J. T. and Lena.

Mooningwanekaaning: That mouthful is Ojibwe for golden-breasted woodpecker. Apparently this island is considered by the Ojibwe to be their "spiritual home," according to the brochure. They, including the golden-breasted woodpeckers, were here long before the fur traders and missionaries. Now why would they name the island after a woodpecker? Go figure.

CHAPTER 17

Workin' the Funk.

"Kids, make yourselves at home. You can take your stuff to the small bedroom. I have to get back to the shop to help Jim. Enjoy."

"What about the cats?"

"What about them?"

"Can they go outside? I wouldn't want to let them out accidentally."

"Michael's two cats, Pete and Lou, are probably outside already; they love hunting along the shoreline and sleeping in the deck chairs. No worries. Gotta go! Happy reunion!" Marie waved as she walked back to Mission Hills Coffee Shop.

My first reaction was that the weathered cedar shake cabin with a great front porch was old and small. Since the cabin was set back from the road and surrounded by mature trees, we couldn't see the addition until we opened the door. And then we saw a wall of windows overlooking beautiful

Lake Superior. The "formal" living room was at the front; I expected it to be dark and "cabiny" since there were so many trees, but I was surprised because Pops had painted everything white, even the beams.

The floors were stained dark and covered with what looked like old, worn Oriental area rugs. A stone fireplace was on the interior wall separating the kitchen/dining/family room addition. The glass wall facing the lake brought in tons of natural light. I definitely felt the beach vibe.

The furniture was upholstered in blue denim and tan linen. Colorful throws and pillows covered the chairs and couches. Pops used one of his huge, colorful birdhouses as the base for a glass-topped coffee table. But it was the kitchen that blew me away.

The cupboards were painted in shades of blue and green with knobs that Pops must have made himself because they were the heads of colorful birds—very funky stuff. I remember Pops being tons of fun, but his artistic flair was just plain awesome.

The first thing Gary did was check out the sound system and Pops's CD collection. Pops liked good old fashioned rock and roll, so Gary found Credence Clearwater Revival and cranked it up. And then we started to dance—all of us, even Lena who ran around barking. It was hard not to be joyful in this beautiful home. Grandma would love this place with its funk and color. J.T. started filming and we started hamming it up. When the music ended, we plopped down into the comfy furniture and rested.

Then my detective brain clicked in.

"Gary, this is a pretty nice and expensive place."

"Ya think?"

"Where did he get all his money?"

"Well, he wasn't living high when he was in St. Cloud. That's for sure. He was working at McDonald's and living in that tiny basement apartment. And then there was the camper. That's hardly luxury living. You don't suppose..." Gary paused long enough for all of us to be thinking the same thing—Pops was guilty of embezzlement.

"But he was exonerated," I said, so wanting to believe in Pops's innocence.

"Maybe that Noah guy was in it with him—a conspiracy—and they split the loot."

"Shut up, J.T.," Gary said with feeling. "I guess we just have to ask him when he gets here. There's probably a logical explanation." So much for joy. I felt like a deflated balloon.

The next few hours dragged by. Seven o'clock

seemed an eternity away. It was like watching Mom in labor or waiting for Grandma to get out of surgery. J.T. and Gary walked outside with Lena and sat on the deck talking. I wasn't in the mood for socializing.

About ten minutes past seven I heard the front door opening. Lena started barking. I ran to meet him. And there he was—bigger than life, the operative word here being bigger. He reminded me of the bear I had encountered earlier, only with auburn hair.

When I remembered Pops, I saw a tall, thin guy with auburn curly hair, clean shaven and rather handsome. Now I was seeing a heavy man with a beard, mustache, and wire-rimmed glasses. Oh, and did I mention the earring? No wonder we didn't get any "hits" on his picture in Bayfield. Ohmigod, who was this guy? Gary must have been reading my mind.

"Hey, man, who are you anyway? What do you want?" Gary didn't even recognize him. How sad was that?

"Gary, I am your dad." He set the takeout down on the coffee table and opened his arms. I started to blubber midway through the bear hug. Pops cried, too. Gary watched, his mouth wide open. J.T. filmed. Lena got her squeaky toy.

"Wow," he said, wiping his eyes. He looked at Lena and J.T.

"Introduce me." He shook hands with J.T. who told him about his film project and then Pops bent down to Lena's height and scratched her behind the ears. She immediately rolled over and begged for a belly rub. I fully believed that dogs were an excellent judge of character. Lena couldn't possibly love an embezzler, could she?

"I imagine you kids have tons of questions. Let's sit down and have some supper. We can talk."

Pops went in to get napkins and silverware. After supper, J.T. excused himself to let us have some privacy.

Two hours later, after telling him about Mom, Bob, Grandma, Ruby, school, my detective work, the letters, his exoneration, Ely, the bear, and finally Bayfield, we finally got down to the "elephant in the room," the real issue, the one that was bothering us.

"Pops, where did you get the money for this beautiful house and the van you drive?" Gary asked.

"You deserve an answer. No, I didn't embezzle the money, if that's what you're thinking. When your mom and I divorced, she got the house, but I legally still owned half. She couldn't afford to buy me out, so she refinanced the house and gave me what she could. In exchange I wouldn't pay child support until I got back on my feet. That and the money I saved from my early jobs gave me enough for the down payment. You wouldn't believe what bad shape the house was in when I bought it. A real 'fixer-upper' as the Realtors like to say. I've spent the last three years making improvements, doing most of the work myself. Then my art business took off. I've been incredibly lucky with new friends and now you kids are here. I couldn't be happier."

"Did you know you had been exonerated?" Gary asked. He sounded angry.'

"Actually, I did. I called Noah and he told me what he'd found when he went back over the books. When Noah confronted the real embezzler, he confessed and I was officially off the hook, but by that time I had signed the divorce papers and I figured you kids were better off without me."

"How could you just walk away?" I said, crying again. "If you knew you were 'off the hook,' why didn't you just come home?"

"Looking back, I realize I made a mistake by leaving you kids. Can you ever forgive me?"

"I think I'll join J.T. on the deck until it's time for bed. This time I'll take the living room couch. Where do you want Toby and J.T.?"

"J.T. can take the guest room and Toby can take my room. I'll use the camper; it's parked in the garage. Just let me get my things. See you in the morning, kids." I was glad Pops didn't push it. Gary left for the deck and I helped Pops clean up. We were all tired.

"He'll come around, Pops." *Maybe Gary'll come around and maybe he won't. What Gary does is his business. I just know I'm in for the duration.* "We've had a lot to process these last few days. Come on, Lena, I'll take you out before we head off for bed."

I went over and gave Pops a kiss good night.

Credence Clearwater Revival: A '60s and '70s band playing Southern rock and roll. Bayous, catfish, po boy sandwiches, Cajun food—all wrapped up in Credence and all in Pops's living room.

CHAPTER 18

Artsy Fartsy Party

By the time we kids rolled out of bed, Pops was long gone. When I went to the kitchen, I discovered our favorite chili cooking in the Crock Pot and a note on the kitchen counter telling us what was available for breakfast (not much), that supper was at five (our favorite chili), and that he could use our help at the studio. He bribed us with homemade muffins, fruit, and juice at the Coffee Shop, his treat. After we showered and dressed, we walked Lena around the island and then to Jim and Marie's.

"I've got an idea, Gary. We could make a sign to put around Lena's neck, advertising Pops's art show."

"Knock yourself out, Toby, but I don't want anything to do with it or him. In fact, I was thinking of leaving today. If Pops thinks he can bribe me with chili..."

"You can't do that, Gary. His show starts tonight and he asked us for help. Can't we at least wait until

135

the show's over? We can leave Monday morning. Come on, Gary. He's our dad, maybe not the dad we wanted, but he's all we got in the dad department. And he needs our help."

"And how many times could we have used his help over the years? Where was he? Making stupid birdhouses. I'm taking the ferry to Bayfield and spending the day over there. J.T., wanna come along?"

"Sure thing. We could help your dad when we get back."

"Yeah, whatever. I'll agree to leaving Monday as long as I don't have to spend a lot of time with him. That chili smelled mighty good."

"He'll be too busy schmoozing with his loyal fans to spend much time with us," J.T. said.

"Aren't you two gonna have some breakfast at Jim and Marie's?" I asked.

"Nah, we'll stop at The Egg Toss for something. Come on, J.T., let's check out the ferry schedule."

"Have fun, Toby," J.T. said.

Gary just walked away. He could be a real jerk sometimes.

"You too," I said.

I get why he's pissed; I was pretty angry myself until I saw Pops, and then all the good memories came back. Grandma's friend Arline called them "memory hugs." When I remembered my broken arm back in grade school, I remembered my Pops holding me and telling me, "All will be well, honey."

I remembered how he smelled and smiled and how much I missed him. And I remembered his delicious Crock Pot chili. He remembered it was our favorite. I was glad he was back in my life. Gary would have to figure it out on his own. Until then I would have brekkie at the Coffee Shop and help Pops get ready for his show. Tonight was the opening. Nothing to wear—story of my life.

Pops loved the Lena as billboard idea, so Lena and I spent the afternoon, wandering the streets wearing these cool signs that Pops made, advertising his whimsical birdhouses and furniture. It reminded me of the silly costumes Freddy and I had to wear at the State Fair two years ago, advertising The Best of the Wurst German food booth. Only Pops's signs were cooler both in temperature and design. The ketchup bottle and the brat and bun were brutal in the heat and humidity.

Lena's sign was much smaller than mine, but very colorful. Her sign simply said:

MW Art Show
Wine and cheese reception: 7 to 9
Mission Coffee House

The MW stood for Michael's Woodworking.

My sign stated the hours for Saturday and Sunday with pictures of his work and past parties superimposed on a large pastel birdhouse, but no one noticed me much because Lena was so adorable. Lots of loves for the pooch. By the time we got back to the house, we were both exhausted. Lena plopped down on the floor with a sigh.

The house smelled delicious. On the table were cool pottery bowls filled with tortilla chips, grated cheese, chopped onions, sour cream and a big bowl of guacamole. Num. I don't know how Gary could resist this.

"Toby, grab a soda and take a load off. I'll join you on the deck. We'll wait for Gary and J.T. to eat."

"Sure thing. Billboard Lena really worked; everybody loved her. I hope we get a good crowd tonight." I sat down in a lavender Adirondack chair.

"I usually do pretty well on opening night. My regular customers show up and bring their friends. Of course, Marie's appetizers are a big draw along with the free wine."

"Do people dress up? 'Cause I don't have any nice clothes to wear."

"Some do, some don't. You'll be fine in your shorts and tees. Honey, you're pretty darn cute just the way you are. 'No need to gild the lily,' to quote Eloise."

"Yeah, Grandma is something else." I paused before I asked, "Do you ever miss the family?"

"Every day I think of you guys." Pops checked his watch. I could tell Pops was getting antsy.

"You think Gary and J.T. will make supper or should we eat without them?"

"What's the latest you can get there?"

"I should be there no later than 6:45. I always try to help Marie set out the refreshments."

"Then I say we eat. If they're late, they can eat appetizers."

After clearing the dishes and putting away the food, I got ready. I changed into my one clean outfit, washed my face, and tried to control my hair. I even added mascara and lip gloss for the occasion. Big whoop.

Pops looked pretty cool in his bright Hawaiian shirt and cargo shorts. I could almost imagine him sitting on the pastel perch of one of his birdhouses.

When we got to the Coffee Shop, there were already people milling about waiting for Michael, the famous artist. Marie had hung white twinkly lights around the gallery, there was music playing by the Bayfield Blues Boys, and the tables had bouquets of fresh flowers. It was very "festive," to use one of Mom's favorite words. Pops schmoozed and I helped Marie ring up sales and wrap birdhouses. By nine we had sold a dozen or more and one large piece of furniture. We all pitched in to clean up.

"Well, gang, it was a good night. Thanks for all your work. Toby and I will see you in the morning. Maybe the guys will join us."

We thought Gary and J.T. were back at the house, but when we got home, the only welcome we got was from Lena.

"What time does the last ferry get to the island?" I asked, beginning to get annoyed and a bit worried.

"It leaves Bayfield at 11:30. I think I'll wait up for them just to make sure they're okay," Pops said as he made a pot of coffee. "Can I get anything for you?"

"Nah, I'm good. I'll stay up with you."

Pops and I were having a nice chat about the evening when the two boys sauntered in around midnight, smelling of beer. J.T. said hello, but Gary headed straight for the deck without even looking at us.

I looked at Pops and all the joy of the evening—

the sales, the food, the compliments, the friends—all disappeared. He looked old, tired and sad.

Pops had the good sense to know there was no talking to Gary under these circumstances, so he gave me a kiss good night and ruffled Lena's fur.

"Good night, son," he whispered to no one.

Gild: To make golden. "To gild the lily" means to add beauty to something already beautiful. It's totally unnecessary. Pops thinks I'm pretty cute as is. No gilding needed. Thanks, Pops.

CHAPTER 19

Now You're Talkin'

We stayed until Monday morning with Gary being incommunicado for most of the weekend. While the rest of us worked our butts off, Gary stayed back at the house or took the ferry to Bayfield and did whatever jerks do in Bayfield.

J.T. was helpful at the Saturday and Sunday shows. He helped carry birdhouses, stock shelves, and clean up.

I did what I could to help Pops, Marie, and Jim with whatever they needed me to do. When I wasn't working at the show, I was walking Lena. It was great hanging out with Pops; it felt like old times.

"I need to talk to you guys," J.T. said as we were beginning to load the car. "I've decided to stay here for another week."

"No way, why would want to do that?" Gary said.

"This place is just awesome. Michael has volunteered his guest room and said he'd help me edit the film in exchange for doing yard work. That's an offer I can't refuse."

"What does he know about editing film?" Gary didn't notice Pops had walked up to the car.

"Well, Gary, I know enough to have made a video ad for my art and put it on You Tube."

"Whatever." Gary said as he slammed the trunk door a bit harder than necessary.

"Kids, I want you to take these to Laura, Eloise, and Ruby." Pops had brought out three of his wonderful birdhouses: the colorful cabin models for Mom and Grandma and an adorable "outhouse" for Ruby. He even added a colorful little bird to put on Ruby's perch.

"And here's the chalet you admired, Toby."

"Thanks, Pops, I love it. I know exactly where it's going in my room." I gave him a big hug.

"Good thing you're not coming with us, J.T. There wouldn't be room," I said, wishing he was coming along. With Gary in such a snotty mood, it was going to be a long ride home.

"Gary, is there a birdhouse you'd like? I still have quite a few left in the gallery. Take your pick."

"Come on, Toby, get in. We've got a five hour drive ahead of us." I gave Pops another hug and shook hands with J.T. "Don't you dare include any footage of me in the woods. You know what I'm talking about." J.T. laughed.

"Thanks for everything, Pops. I'll try to visit during Fall Break. I'll bet it's awesomely beautiful here. Maybe I can talk Grandma into driving since Gary is being such a brat."

"I'd love to see Eloise; she always made me laugh. Have a good trip, kids. I loved having you here."

"Bye, Pops." As soon as we got into the car and started driving, I let Gary have it. "You could have at least answered his question. I can't believe how rude you were. And don't you dare say 'whatever.'"

Gary was silent during the ferry ride and he was silent all the way to Duluth. I tried to start a few conversations, but it was like talking to the rocky shoreline of Lake Superior. So I gave up and let him "Stew in his own juices," to quote Grandma.

When we reached Duluth, we stopped for lunch and a potty break for both Lena and me. I called Mom to let her know we'd be home in a few hours.

"Gary, wanna talk to Mom?"

He shook his head. "Sorry, Mom, Gary has an extreme case of Assholeitis and can't talk to anyone except J.T. and since J.T. stayed on with Pops for a week, he won't talk to anybody. If he gets over it, I'll let you know. Right now, though, it looks terminal. I'll let him know you're concerned. I do hope it's not contagious."

I remembered reading in Maya Angelou's book *I Know Why the Caged Bird Sings* that she didn't talk for years. That could be Gary.

Gary used to bet me that I couldn't refrain from talking for an hour. The longest I was silent was forty-five minutes. Riding home from Bayfield, was an all time record in the Great Mute-Off.

Just outside of Wyoming, MN I couldn't stand it any more. "Gary, I need to use the bathroom. I don't think I can hold it."

"Not again. Didn't you use the bathroom in Duluth?"

"Yeah, but my tummy's upset. Pull over."

As soon as we pulled over to the side of the road and the car had come to a complete stop, I reached over and pulled out the keys.

"What are you doing?"

"We need to talk and this is all I could think of. I'll give you the keys back when we've talked about stuff. I need to know that we're okay—that you and I are okay. Nothing to do with Pops. Are we okay?" I asked again.

"Yes, Toby, you and I are okay. I'm not mad at you—well, I am mad a little—but I'm mostly mad at Pops. When he said he knew that he had been exonerated, that was it for me. He could have come home, but he chose not to. I just can't wrap my brain around that. And I don't know how you can."

"I know how hurt you are. I am too, but when I was with him these past few days, it felt right. I was happy to be a part of his life again. I saw his passion for his art, his friends, his new life. Without a family, he connected with who he really wanted to be and that wasn't an accountant with family obligations. He wanted freedom. I get that. I feel that way every summer when school's out. Pops just chose not to go back to school."

"That's exactly what I don't get, Toby. He chose freedom over us. It's as simple as that. And right now I can't forgive him. Maybe I will somewhere down the line; maybe I won't."

"Now it's my turn to say 'whatever' because I will support you whatever you decide. I promise."

"Okay, Sis, now can I have the keys back? I really wanna get home to see everyone."

"Me too." Lena barked: her version of "Me three." "Since we're okay, let's hear some grunge, Bro."

"Now you're talkin.'"

Incommunicado: Unwilling or unable to communicate. Gary deliberately chose silence, but that silence communicated volumes. Maya Angelou (born April 4, 1928): African American poet, activist, and author. In 9th grade we were forced to read *I Know Why the Caged Bird Sings,* an autobiography of her childhood in Stamps, Arkansas, and I loved it! She was a strong girl who became an even stronger woman.

CHAPTER 20

Home again, home again, jiggity jig

When we got home, the welcoming committee was assembled on the porch: Grandma, Mom, Bob, Ruby, Freddy and Watson. Watson waddled down the steps to greet his sister who was very excited to see him. The next few minutes were pure doggy joy: sniffing, chasing, and peeing.

"Ree," Ruby squealed as she ran to hug her big brother. He bent down, picked her up, and tossed her in the air. I could see that the Rugrat might just be the medicine Gary needed. If I could bottle Ruby's sweet energy, I might be a rich girl.

"What, am I chopped liver? Come here, Rugrat, and give me a sticky hug. I've missed you." She ran over to me and gave me a big sloppy kiss. Then she put her chubby little hands on my cheeks and gave me one of her famous butterfly kisses.

Plopping down on the grass, she said, "Toby, play little piggy with me." She took off her sandals and wiggled her little piggies.

"Wanna play little piggy with me," Freddy said with a grin. Is it possible that my best pal, Freddy, had got even more handsome?

"Nah, I'm good with a hug." It felt wonderful to be home and in Freddy's arms. "What's for supper?" Gary asked and everybody laughed.

"I've taken care of that with my lasagna and fixins," Grandma said to a round of applause. Mom went up to Gary, took his hand and said, "How are you feeling, honey?"

"Good, now that I'm home." When Gary and I were walking back to the car for a load, he said to me, "I can't believe you told Mom I was an..."

I interrupted him, "Gary, the line was dead when I made that comment. Mom was just worried about you. Nope, your incurable disease was just between you and me. Glad the symptoms have gone away."

Gary grinned.

We unloaded the car, distributed bird houses, much to Ruby's delight, and went inside to feast. Mom and Grandma had gone all out. The smell of lasagna in the oven was mouth-watering. The table was set with our good dishes, tablecloth, matching napkins, and a centerpiece of fresh flowers. A beautiful tossed salad and a bowl of garlic bread also adorned the table. It was Thanksgiving in August.

Gary and I entertained everyone with road trip tales; the favorite, of course, was my pooping in the woods and encountering a bear. Grandma laughed so hard she spit out her wine. I looked at Ruby with tomato sauce all over her face and sundress, Bob and Mom sharing loving looks, Gary and Freddy talking and laughing. *This is my family and I love them.* I was filled with gratitude for all of them, even Pops.

Nobody asked much about Pops and neither Gary nor I volunteered much information, other than the obvious—his art and where he lived and worked.

I spent the following week doing chores: washing clothes, writing thank-you notes to Betty in St. Cloud, Sherry and Luca in Ely, and Jim and Marie on Madeline Island, and baby-sitting the Rugrat.

Gary and I decided to thank Noah Swanson in person for helping Pops. Nice man, a bit nerdy, but nice. He had the guts to face his boss with the mistake he'd made. I told him about Pops's new life and he seemed pleased that things turned out.

J.T. sent Lena's photos to us so we could forward them to Sam and Carrie in St. Cloud. He promised a copy of the documentary *Finding Pops* in the next few weeks. That should be a hoot.

Gary went to work at the State Fair in The Best of the Wurst German food booth. He would be exhausted, dirty and smelly for the next twelve days, but he was saving money for college.

As a new high school student, I could hardly wait to get my schedule. I wanted to know my teachers, my rooms, if my friends and I shared any classes. I got my schedule the Friday before Patty's party. I immediately called my BF.

"Freddy, who do you have for English 10?

"How would I know, Toby?"

"Check your mail, Doofus." I waited and then I heard a whoop.

"Me too! Mrs. Trattles, we're back!

Now for Patty's awesome party where I got my first real kiss, but I'm not one to kiss and tell, at least not to anyone outside the family.

> *Dear Pops,*
>
> *Have I got lots to tell you ...Patty Washington had this awesome party last Saturday night; all of the Pearls were there, but there's one very special Pearl. You remember our neighbor, Freddy Galvin? Well, he's my business partner and best friend...*

Pops and I wrote to each other every week; no e-mails, no texting, just real, honest, handwritten letters. This time Mom didn't confiscate them. At the end of each letter, he would ask me to say hi to Gary and the rest of the family.

Gary continued to vacillate about Pops; one minute he was still angry and the next he was reading woodworking books and examining how Pops constructed the birdhouses. It was late in September when I heard pounding in the basement and when I went to investigate, I found Gary making a doll house for Ruby. Maybe the apple doesn't fall far from the tree.

Speaking of apples, Grandma and I headed to Bayfield to check out the very famous Bayfield fall apple festival. I suspect we'll take the ferry to Madeline Island to check out a certain artist. We have an idea for Mom's Christmas present: we want Pops to make a birdhouse just like our one hundred year old farmhouse in Merriam Park.

Gary and I went searching for our father and we found him, but we found something else as well. We discovered our love for each other. We also discovered we had a pretty cool stepdad who wasn't going to disappear while going out for milk.

Vacillate: To go back and forth on an issue, namely Pops. It took quite a few years for Gary to come to terms with Pops and his decision to leave the family, but he finally took the leap and visited Pops after he graduated from St. Cloud State University. He spent the summer with Pops fine tuning his doll house making skills. Go figure.

EPILOGUE

THE
QUARRY
MURDERS

TOBY MARTIN

THE QUARRY MURDERS
BY TOBY MARTIN

Swimming, parties, sex, rock 'n' roll, Janet Cavell just loved summers at the quarries. They're the main reason she enrolled in summer school at St. Cloud State University, a prestigious party school. What she didn't plan on was being murdered along with three other coeds found dead "on the rocks."

> "*A DELICIOUSLY COMPLEX CAST* of engaging characters led by Detective Deanna Duress who captivates with her wit, intelligence, and naughtiness. A delightful combination of humor and horror as the murders pile up in St. Cloud."
> —Eloise Tobias, author of *Sassy and Seventy*.

ISBN 978-1-61836-274-2A

51895

Available From
www.cambridgebooks.us
www.writewordsinc.com
or your favorite bookstore.
$18.95

cambridge books

Write Words Inc. Cambridge, MD 21613

PRAISE FOR TOBY MARTIN

The Quarry Murders
by Toby Martin

"I STAYED UP ALL NIGHT to finish this remarkable book by a remarkable woman. Ms. Martin has grabbed her audience, jerked us around, abused and amused us, and we love her for it. The St. Paul setting was spot on, the plot twisty, the characters likable. It doesn't get any better than this."
— Lenore Trattles, author of the best seller *Delicate Dames, Inc.*

"TOBY MARTIN, LOCAL GAL, hits it out of the park with her first novel. Filled with fun, well-developed characters and a detective who surprises and delights, this novel is a must read for summer."
— *St Paul Pioneer Press*

"MAN, IF I HAD KNOWN about the quarries, I sure wouldn't have spent so much time swimming there. This is one scary read."
— Gary Martin, St. Cloud State University graduate

"WITH A RELAXED, almost slangy style, Ms. Martin has created her own little world filled with deception, betrayal, and murder. Detective Duress bristles with energy, curiosity, and sexuality, giving the book an edgy quality. If this were a movie, you sure wouldn't leave for popcorn."
— Jacob Thomas Kirkowski, award winning film-maker of *It Still Hurts: How Divorce Affects Adult Children*

THE QUARRY MURDERS

by Toby Martin

𝕮𝖆𝖒𝖇𝖗𝖎𝖉𝖌𝖊 𝕭𝖔𝖔𝖐𝖘

an imprint of
WriteWords, Inc.
CAMBRIDGE, MD 21613

𝕮𝖆𝖒𝖇𝖗𝖎𝖉𝖌𝖊 𝕭𝖔𝖔𝖐𝖘 is a subsidiary of:

Write Words, Inc.
2934 Old Route 50
Cambridge, MD 21613

ISBN   978-1-61386-274-2A

Fax: 410-221-7510

Bowker Standard Address Number: 254-0304

Dedication

This one's for you, Fred.

Acknowledgements

I started writing mystery stories when I was twelve years old under the tutelage of Mrs. Lenore Trattles, my seventh grade English teacher. Without her, this book would have stayed trapped in my twisted brain, screaming for release. She also broke me of a really really bad adverb addiction.

Thanks to Bob Murphy, my wonderfully supportive stepdad and one of St. Paul's finest, who helped with the forensic and procedural details of a murder investigation.

As always thanks to my family—Grandma, Mom, Bob, Pops, Gary, and Ruby—your love and support are greatly appreciated.

And to Fred, my loyal foil, friend, and husband, you deserve a medal for loving me when I was most unlovable.

The End
Really...

ABOUT THE AUTHOR

Barbara Grengs is a retired English teacher who reads, writes, gardens, and knits. She currently resides in Roseville, Minnesota with her two dogs.

Real Acknowledgements

Since the Toby series is officially finished, I need to thank many people.

Jim and Marie Noha: the real life owners of the Mission Hills Coffee Shop who graciously allowed me to borrow their identities.

Orrin Miller: an artist from Alexandria, who creates colorful birdhouses. When I saw them, I knew exactly what kind of artist I wanted Michael to be.

Noah Swanson: character auction winner for my local Rotary club. Real life Noah is working in Salt Lake City as an MBA and is a new daddy. I hope he and his wife will read the books together with their boy.

Jacob Thomas Kirkowski: another character auction winner for my favorite nonprofit, Northeast Youth and Family Services. When I had lunch with this vibrant preteen, he had his character pretty much nailed: "I want to be older, taller, a filmmaker and I don't want any romance." No cooties for J.T.

Sue Holthaus: my dear friend, former colleague, and my first reader. We taught English together from 1969-2001. Go figure. She has been honest, but kind, thorough and helpful. Plus, we laugh our butts off together; you can't beat a sense of humor in a first reader.

Judy Bergerson: extraordinary cover artist and old high school friend. Her covers, in my opinion, make the Toby books. I will miss having her read the manuscript and zone in on the visuals that enhance and summarize the books. Brilliant, girlfriend

Arline Chase: my publisher and editor, who decided to take a chance on an old English teacher. She has helped me fulfill a lifelong dream and I couldn't be more grateful.

Lee Johnson: my high school sweetie, who has miraculously re-entered my life. I feel very comfortable stealing his jokes and his puns, word slut that I am. Old love is good love.

Henry Warren Andersson: my dear grandson who suggested that the final Toby book include a road trip. Always trust literary suggestions from your grandchildren.

Carrie Andersson: my sweet daughter and confidante who was always willing to listen, support, and encourage. You and Henry are the best.

Minneapolis Writers' Workshop: my sounding board for early versions of the first few books. Your comments were always respected and appreciated. Okay, some were ignored.

Friends, family, and students: my support, my inspirations, my heroes. You have endured many readings and signings, going well beyond.

Toby Martin: my protagonist, my pal, my literary daughter. I will miss you.

Thanks to all of you.

If I've forgotten anyone, my sincere apologies. I'm old.

31774669R00096

Made in the USA
San Bernardino, CA
20 March 2016